T0090505

AN ELFIN SERIES--BOOK 1

Martha Cabados

authorHOUSE

AuthorHouse™
1663 Liberty Drive
Bloomington, IN 47403
www.authorhouse.com
Phone: 833-262-8899

Published by AuthorHouse 06/07/2023

ISBN: 979-8-8230-0940-9 (sc)
ISBN: 979-8-8230-0941-6 (e)

Library of Congress Control Number: 2023910270

Print information available on the last page.

CONTENTS

ACKNOWLEDGEMENT

This acknowledgement comes from the sands of time for a wonderful, caring man, Clement C. Moore who wrote **'TWAS THE NIGHT BEFORE CHRISTMAS** for his daughter one Christmas Eve. A poem that has dwelt in the hearts of children, young and old, since it was first published on December 23, 1823. His beautiful prose is the reason I write Christmas stories for all the little children around the world.

Contact Author
Email: southernladyx2007@yahoo.com

DEDICATION

This book is dedicated to my devoted husband, Rudy, who endured hours of listening and for his encouragement and participation. I also dedicate this book to my children, grandchildren and great grandchildren, too many to mention but they know who they are

In Loving Memory of
Our son,
William L. Bentley

1

Santa's Village

… …… VISIONS OF SUGARPLUMS DANCED IN THEIR HEADS

Snow, snow, snow and more snow in the Elf Kingdom at the North Pole. Elro gazed out of his window and wondered how they were going to get to Santa's toy shop. The snow was over their heads and they would be buried alive if they tried to leave. Elro knew Santa needed their help to manufacture millions of toys for the little children of the world, plus he was anxious to see his friend, Elendeth. He sighed and turned away.

Elro was ready to leave the Kingdom for a taste of freedom. Today was the first day of October so he would have three months of it in the

Village. Working for Santa in his Toy Shop was one privilege granted to the elves by Commander Alberi; besides, working in the toy shop, he would be with his best friend, Elendeth.

Elendeth had been left on Santa's doorstep when he was born. Santa took him in and eventually adopted him. He was quite tall for an elf and some of the others gave him a nickname of "Stiltz." He was not a part of the Kingdom, however; there were some rules he had to obey just because he was an elf and Santa had to agree to them with the Commander when he was adopted.

The next morning Elro was awakened by a loud clatter. He jumped out of bed and looked out the window and Santa was on his snow plow throwing snow everywhere. He jumped up and down with excitement. He and the other elves would be able to start work tomorrow. A few of the elves looked at their job as a drudgery, but not Elro; it was the best time of the year for him. *Wow, each day, for three months away from the Kingdom. Getting away from the Kingdom and its Ruler, Commander Alberi, was a blessing, he thought.*

Elro was so excited he couldn't sleep that night. He wanted to see his friend and be near the Clauses. He was up at dawn fixing his lunch for the day. He returned to his room and looked out the window. Santa had finished and there was a pathway to his village. Elro waited patiently for the other elves to wake up so they could leave.

As the elves awoke, each fixed his own lunch and within an hour they were out the door and on their way to Santa's Village. One by one, the elves trampled through the path carrying a sack lunch. Their hours in Santa's workshop were long, but with all the hustle, bustle and excitement, most of them loved working for him. They were happy to be away from the Elf Kingdom even for a day because they weren't under strict rules of the Commander.

When they were within sight of the Village, Elro broke into a run. When he reached the toy shop, he flung the door open and saw his friend at his station working on music boxes. "Hey, Elendeth, we're here to start work and I'm so happy to see you. I love being here with you and having a taste of freedom."

Elen looked up and smiled. "I'm real happy to see you too, Elro. It's been a long time. Welcome back, my friend. What a great feeling to have you around."

The toy shop was huge. Santa had built thirty work stations; one for each elf. Posted at their station, were their orders for each project they were going to make. The walls were painted with decorated Christmas trees, dolls, trains, skates, and anything that resembled the holiday and gifts for children. Christmas music was piped into the shop to keep the season alive. The elves loved it and they loved Santa dearly.

After each elf had reached their station and read the poster of their duties, you could hear engines running, the pounding of hammers and the sanding and grinding of wood. A whiff of wood and plastic was in the air. Some of the projects were larger and took longer to make but when they were finished, all of them were painted or glossed to a high luster. When finished, they were set on shelves that were attached to their station or put into a large room, depending on their size.

When it was time for a break, a bell sounded. The elves went to the lunch room, had a snack and enjoyed conversation with the others. Santa could hear them laughing and yelling on their break. He smiled and thought of how blessed he was to have the elves working for him. He paid them generously every week for their work.

Just before dusk fell, the elves cleaned their station and left for the Kingdom bidding Elendeth goodbye.

When Elendeth finished cleaning his station he headed directly to Santa's library until dinner was called. Mrs. Claus had taught him to read and write along with many other subjects so he was well versed on most anything. He read and studied how to build houses, barns or whatever a person or animal needed for shelter. As he read, he learned many things about other countries and other people in different parts of the world. It seemed as though he couldn't learn enough about the world around him. He lusted for more knowledge.

Elendeth was happy and at home with the Clauses. He never dwelt on knowing what his real family was like or wanting to be near them. There were times however, that he wondered what it would be like to have a brother and sister but it was a passing thought. He was content and loved Santa and Mrs. Claus with all his heart.

Elendeth dreamed of Santa letting him travel with him on Christmas Eve but he hadn't approached him about it yet. He wanted to see the world. He wanted to see other children. He questioned everything and was willing to learn.

Mrs. Claus called Elendeth to supper. He sat at the table and murmured a prayer then began to eat. When he lifted his cup for a drink, he turned it in his hand. "What is this cup made of Santa?"

"It's silver."

"Silver?" asked Elendeth. "Why is it made with silver?"

"Well," said Santa, "in the early days, silver played a big part in people's lives after its discovery. Cups and steins were made of silver to drink from because it purified water. The same is true of the utensils you eat with. Many things were made with silver after its discovery. Beautiful things like jewelry for the ladies, fruit platters and fancy bowls and small items for decoration in the home. The only other thing to drink from was something made of tin, but tin would rust over a period of time. When they used tin, they always put a silver coin in the bottom to purify the water to keep infection away. Glass came into being thousands of years ago but it was a luxury and most people couldn't afford it so they preferred silver over any other vessel to drink from,

"Whoa, that's very interesting, Santa. I have something I've wanted to ask you for a long time. My question is; would you let me travel with you on Christmas Eve this year? I would love to see other countries and would especially like to see other children."

Santa sat quiet for a moment stirring his tea and pondering an answer. Soon he looked up at Elendeth. "No," he said. "You are much too young. When you are older I will consider it."

"All right, Santa," said Elendeth lowering his head in disappointment.

Elendeth lay in bed that night wondering how he could manage a trip with Santa on Christmas Eve even though Santa told him no. Temptation was so great to see the world but he knew he was too tall to fit into his sack of toys. There had to be another way, he thought.

After a few days had passed, Elendeth decided to sneak into Santa's office. It was off limits to him but he had to find a way to go without Santa being wise to it. When he stepped into his office he noticed a huge vat in a corner and wondered why it was there.

He quickly glanced around and spotted a ladder on the side of the vat that went to the top. He ran to it and began climbing. When he got to the top he heard Santa's footsteps and lost his balance and fell in. As he fell through the softness of the product, he sunk to the bottom having to close his eyes and hold his breath; he fumbled around, worried, feeling for another ladder to climb out. There was none. He began getting scared but kept searching to find a way out. Finally he felt something round and latched onto it and started climbing as well as he could. By the time he got to the top, Santa was gone, *"Thank goodness,"* he thought. He gasped for air. It felt good to breathe again.

When Elendeth grabbed for the rim of the vat something was dreadfully wrong. He was having trouble grasping it. He looked down at his hand with wide eyes; then looked at the other. Why were they so small? He was able to climb over the rim but the ladder he had climbed onto was much bigger now. He pondered for a moment and realized he had fallen into the vat of Santa's magical dust and it had shrunk him. Once he was down the ladder, he ran to the coat closet afraid; not knowing what to do but to wait to see if the dust wore off so he could return to his normal size.

While in the closet the strange happening dawned on him. Oh my gosh, I know what Santa's secret is now. I can use this to hide in Santa's sack. He grabbed both hands full of the dust and placed them in his pockets before he returned to his normal size.

Once down, he ran quickly into the coat closet hoping the magic dust would wear off and he would return to his normal size. While he waited, a thought came to him. *The dust must wear off, because Santa is as big as he's always been so he waited calmly for it to wear off.*

Minutes later Elendeth had returned to his normal size. He quietly slipped out of the closet and returned to the toy shop. His head was abuzz with thoughts of what he would be able to see as he traveled with Santa. He was excited to think of seeing the world and other children that were different than him.

With snow over their heads, it was difficult for anyone to go outside to play or travel any-where, but a path had been made to the stables to feed the reindeer.

One weekend Elro burst through the door at the toy shop. Elendeth was at his station working. "Elro, what are you doing here? How did you get away from Commander Alberi?'

Elro laughed. "It wasn't easy, my friend, but I'm going to enjoy every minute I can with you."

Elendeth sighed. "You're taking a big chance, Elro. If the Commander finds you gone and he comes looking for you, it'll mean big trouble for you."

Elro looked at Elendeth and shrugged his shoulders. "You have never lived under Commander Alberi's control. With him around it's like living under his finger. You have no freedom of your own. It's worth a chance to break away now and then and especially to see a friend."

Elendeth shook his head and smiled. "I realize the temptation to get away, but if you're caught, you'll have to pay for it big time."

"I know, but paying for it even for one week is worth spending a day with you. Hey, let's go out and stir up some mischief."

Elendeth looked at Elro and gave him a wistful smile. "What kind of mischief is that, Elro?"

"Let's race to the candy cane light and back."

"Nah, I'm trying to get ahead on the music boxes. Christmas is getting close. Besides, the snow is too deep; we can't race with snow over our heads."

"Oh, come on party pooper, let's have some fun. The reindeer can fly. I need to have some fun and relaxation. It will only be for a few minutes."

Elendeth looked at Elro and saw the desperation in his eyes. "Okay, okay, but not for long. I promised Santa I'd try to get ahead with the music boxes because it's getting so close to Christmas."

"Yahoo, let's go," yelled Elro.

Elendeth put on his winter coat and grabbed his magic wand as they ran out the door heading for the stables. "I get dibs on Prancer," shouted Elro. When they reached the stables, Elro led Prancer out of her stall. Elendeth chose Dasher because he thought he would be faster.

They began racing back and forth between the candy cane light and stable but Elendeth lost interest so he waved his wand and soon they were on a merry-go-round in the air. After going around for a while Elro called out to Elendeth. "Hey, stop the world and let me off, I think Prancer is getting dizzy."

Elendeth stopped the merry-go-round and they flew back to the toy shop. When Prancer landed she stumbled and fell. Elro jumped off and was attempting to help her get up on her feet. When Elendeth landed, he rushed over to Elro.

"What happened, Elro?" he asked.

"I guess she got too dizzy and stumbled."

"Let's get her into the stable to take care of her," said Elendeth. They tugged and pulled for some time before they were able to get her up. When they finally managed to get her on her feet, she limped as they led her to her stall, in the stable. Elendeth felt her ankle and it was beginning to swell. "Oh, golly, Elro, we're in a heap of trouble. Run outside and bring in snow so I can pack it around her ankle." Elro kept Elendeth supplied with snow to pack around Prancer's ankle to keep the swelling down.

As Elro watched Elendeth, he worried. "I sure hope Santa doesn't find out about this." Those words no sooner came out of Elro's mouth when Santa appeared.

"Find out what?" asked Santa.

Shocked to hear Santa, the elves looked up. "Oh, Santa, we were racing Prancer and Dasher when Prancer fell and hurt her ankle," said Elro.

"You did what? With Christmas only a few weeks away, you were racing them? I can't believe you boys did this."

"I'm trying to cure it, Santa, with ice and my magic wand," said Elendeth.

"Oh, fiddlesticks, that's nonsense. You could cure my figure before you cure her ankle," said Santa as he turned to leave.

"But it's worth a try, Santa. We'll work with her every day," said Elro.

Santa threw his arms up in desperation and disgust and walked away. Elendeth and Elro looked at each other and shrugged their shoulders.

"Run and get more snow, Elro. Keep me in supply."

Elro picked up the bucket and ran to get snow and brought it back to Elendeth. "What does the snow do, Elendeth?"

"It works as an ice pack and causes the blood vessels to constrict and limit blood flow to the injured area. It keeps the swelling down and acts as a pain relief by numbing the nerve endings in the area. We just have to keep the ice pack on it and hopefully she will be able to lead Santa's sled on Christmas Eve."

"That's very interesting. I don't know where you get all your smarts, but you are good. How long do you have to leave the pack on?"

Elendeth smiled. "It'll be left on her ankle for about twenty minutes at a time. Once I stop the treatment, the veins will dilate and blood rushes into the area and the nutrients rush back to heal the ankle. Everything I've learned is from Santa and Mrs. Claus and through their library."

"Wow," said Elro. "You are so fortunate to have that blessing."

"Yes, I am. When I'm not making music boxes, I'm in the library reading books; I practically live there. I think I've read just about every book in his library." Elendeth looked at Elro and grinned.

"Well, all I can say is, you're certainly a lifesaver, Elendeth. I hope we can heal it before Christmas Eve."

Elro stayed over, hoping Commander Alberi wouldn't miss him and worked through the night on Prancer with Elen. They kept her lying still and off her feet until the next morning. They slept in the stable all night, getting up occasionally to care for Prancer's ankle. "Do you think she'll be all right by Christmas Eve?" asked Elro.

"I certainly hope so," said Elendeth. "Give me hand, Elro. Let's get her on her feet." Elendeth placed a halter on Prancer and coaxed her to stand. He led her around the stable to monitor her walking. "She's doing better but I still need to work with her and keep her off her feet."

Elendeth worked every day on music boxes at his station in the toy shop. At night, he spent his time in the stable with Prancer, hoping she would heal by Christmas Eve. Elro had left to go back to the Kingdom before he was found missing.

Santa went to the stables every day to check on her progress since it was only a few days before their journey across the world.

2

Left Behind

As Christmas Eve got closer, Elendeth was getting more and more excited. He was still plotting to go with Santa by using his magic dust. He planned on climbing into Santa's sack of toys after it had been packed and sprinkle himself with the magic dust. Hopefully everything would go as planned.

By the time Christmas Eve was upon them, Santa knew he wouldn't be able to use Prancer so he replaced her with Rudolph at the front of the sleigh beside Dasher. The sleigh and the reindeer were ready for their trip. All Santa had to do was to load the sack of toys into the sleigh before he left on his trip that night.

After Elendeth helped Santa pack his sack with toys, Santa left the toy shop to dress for his annual duties across the world for all the little children. While he was gone, Elendeth fetched the magic dust from his hideaway; climbed into the bag of toys and sprinkled himself with magic dust. Immediately, he was shrunk to the size of a doll.

After Santa dressed in his red velvet suit, he went to the toy shop, picked up the sack of toys and took it outside placing it carefully in the back of the sled. He bid Mrs. Claus goodbye and they were off into the starry night. Elendeth could feel himself rising into the sky. *Oh, my gosh I wonder if Santa feels this way every year. It's so exciting. I can't wait to see the world and the little children living there.*

Since he was near the top of the sack, he was able to peek out occasionally. The sky was a deep blue and stars twinkled like someone was turning them off and on. They looked the size of a baseballs because they seemed closer than they were on Earth. It was a lot cooler since they were higher and it seemed to be much darker. *I guess that's why Santa always wore his red suit and hat. It kept him warm, he thought.*

Elendeth could hear Santa talk to the reindeer and give them directions. Since he was closer to other countries, they were his first stops. Elendeth had decided he didn't care to see any other places other than the United States because they were above the equator and much colder. Besides, he had heard that the United States was the biggest jewel of all the other countries and that's what wanted to see.

The movement of the sleigh intrigued Elendeth. He could feel and hear the air rushing by him. *We must be traveling over one hundred miles per minute, he guessed but he felt safe. After all, Santa has been making this trip for hundreds of years and will do it again and again for hundreds of years more and he has never had an accident to his understanding and probably never will.*

Santa's stops happened frequently. Each time, he grabbed the sack of toys and if they had a chimney, that was the way he chose to enter the home. He worked swiftly filling every stocking and placing gifts under the tree for every child. Most children left cookies and milk for Santa because they knew he had a long and tiring trip to make around the world.

After he took a break, he turned and placed his finger aside of his nose and rose up the chimney. Elendeth could feel the squeeze as they returned to the rooftop.

Did Santa ever make his trips around the world without magic dust, Elendeth wondered. Where does he get it or how does he make it? Santa is a mystery, not only to me but to all the little children of the world but they don't question it because they love him and all he stands for. I don't think I'll ever regret this trip with Santa. I'm learning so much, not only about Santa but about the world and his travel Elendeth thougtht.

Once back in the sleigh and after many, many stops, Santa called out to his team of reindeer. "Mexico is out next stop, team, then we head *for* America."

America! That's where I want to go. He began to get butterflies the size of buzzards in the middle of his stomach. He was excited but scared at the same time because he would be getting out of Santa's sack once they entered a house. Elendeth was trying to prepare himself for this big and unknown adventure but he wasn't sure it was working because he still had those doggone butterflies in the pit of his stomach. He crouched down lower in the sack of toys because it was beginning to empty with all the stops that had been made. He didn't want Santa to find him when he reached in the bag. He kicked back and waited for the next stop.

"On Dasher and Rudolph, our first stop in America will be in Foley, Alabama. We have two children, a boy and a girl, to leave gifts for," called out Santa.

When Elendeth heard Santa, he became eager to learn it was a boy and a girl; he would get to see both. When they arrived, he could feel the sled land on the rooftop. Then down the chimney they went. While Santa's back was turned, Elendeth slipped out of the bag and ran to each room looking for the children. He couldn't find them. He continued to look then spotted steps leading upward in the family room. *Oh, no how am I going to get up there? Those are like a mountain to climb. I'll have to wait till I return to my normal size.*

He glanced over to see if Santa was still working and he was so he slipped into a closet and waited. When he returned to his normal size, he left the closet and quickly climbed the stairs. The first room he entered he saw a beautiful girl. Her hair was the color of honey, with long ringlets cascading down her shoulders. He was enchanted with her beauty and stood looking at her face. She looked perfect in every way. Her ears were quite small, nothing like his. She had a cute turned-up nose and dimples alongside her mouth. He gazed in wonder at her beauty then he remembered Santa working downstairs so he went to the next room.

When he entered the second room, he saw the boy. He noticed he was tall and had a muscular body; it was nothing like his frail body. His hair was light brown and wavy. He was handsome with nice features and an olive colored skin. His ears were small like that of the girl. He studied him for a short moment then remembered Santa so he rushed down the stairs.

When he got down to the first floor, he looked around for Santa but he was gone. He panicked. He rushed through the house looking for him then rushed outside to see if Santa was still on the roof, but he was nowhere in sight.

He went back inside the house out of the cold, shaking not only with fear, but also of being cold. He spotted a huge overstuffed chair and walked over and sat down concerned how he was going to get back home. He was warm and comfortable so it wasn't long before he was fast asleep. He was awakened by a clatter of feet and children yelling while running down the stairs. He jumped up and spotted a closet and ducked into it to hide.

The children were screaming with excitement when they saw what Santa had left. For Cody, he had left a guitar and for Lela, he had left a doll with a trunk full of doll clothes. Soon, the parents joined the children and Bob began handing out presents.

Elendeth heard the excitement in the children's voices as their father passed out gifts and they opened them. He shrunk deeper into the closet to avoid anyone hearing the chatter of his teeth and his deep breathing while he waited for the right moment to escape. After the gifts were opened, and everything had calmed down, the parents left the room to start breakfast.

Cody was strumming on his new guitar and his sister was dressing her new doll when the door to the closet creaked and the children looked up and saw a boy dart from the closet dashing toward the sliding glass door. He opened it and slammed it shut heading for the forest of trees.

The children jumped up and barreled outside in their pajamas in hot pursuit. "Hey, wait," called Cody, an adventurous boy. "It's unsafe in the forest. Stop, please stop."

"Hurry, Cody, run faster," yelled Lela, trailing behind him.

As the boy entered the forest, he felt his stomach tighten. His heart pounded with panic but with fear as his fuel, he was forced to speed up his stride leaving the children behind.

"Dagnabit, he's too fast," grumbled Cody kicking at a clump of dirt sending it skyward. They turned and trudged back home looking over their shoulders occasionally hoping to see the boy but only saw the forest of trees.

Lela looked up at Cody with concern. "Shall we tell Mommy and Daddy about the boy?" she asked.

"No, not now, maybe later, I need to think about it."

Rolling her eyes, she asked, "Well what are we going to do? Can't we at least take him food and warm clothing?"

"I'm not sure," said Cody shrugging his shoulders. "We'd be in deep doo-doo if Dad ever found out."

Later, when the children were called to dinner, Cody squirmed in his chair and looked at his father and asked. "Dad, may we go into the forest tomorrow?'

His father looked up. "Why do you ask?"

"I love the forest, Dad. I love the smell of pines and watching them sway in the breeze. The sound of the rippling brook is awesome. I like to watch the rabbits and squirrels scampering about too. It's a whole different world in there," said Cody.

"You're still too young. There are three hundred acres of trees and wild animals out there. You'd get lost without a compass. It's not safe. Besides, I haven't forgotten the last time you went in without permission. Don't even think about it," said his father.

"Yes, Dad, said Cody." Disappointed, Cody looked at Lela and lowered his head.

3

A Secret Plan

Later that night, Lela tip-toed to Cody's room and quietly knocked on his door and entered.

"Have you decided what we're going to do, Cody?" she asked. "Are we going into the forest to look for the boy or not?"

"I don't know what to do, you heard what Dad said." Cody sat in deep thought for a moment.

Lela broke the silence and threw her arms up in desperation. "I did hear, Cody, but what about the boy? He could starve or an animal might kill him. Doesn't that make it a matter of life or death for him?"

Cody looked into his sister's troubled eyes and marveled at her bravery. He thought about it. "Okay, okay, we'll flip a coin. Heads we go; tails we stay."

"Goody, goody, I'll get the coin." Lela ran to her room, grabbed her piggy bank, and shook it until a coin dropped. Snatching it up, she ran back to Cody's room. "Here's a quarter, Cody."

Cody took the coin and flipped it onto a brightly colored hand-made quilt. They leaned forward to see what the boy's fate would be.

"Heads it is, we'll start packing tomorrow," said Cody.

"All right, Cody, I can't wait to find him."

After their parents left for work the next morning, Lela began searching for items of survival then she made sandwiches of peanut butter and honey. She wrapped them in waxed paper and returned to Cody's room. "I'm bringing yarn and scissors too. We'll need them to mark the trees to find our way back home."

Cody was amazed at his little sister's insight. "Good thinking little sis. "I'll bring Dad's ax too. We may need it for protection or cutting through thickets." He ran out to the workshop and grabbed his Dad's ax and picked up a can of wasp spray then rushed back to the house.

"What's the can for?" asked Lela.

"Wasps, or other dangers. What have you packed, Lela?"

"One of your old coats, a blanket, sandwiches, a flashlight, and matches.

"Good, I've packed clothes too, along with a blanket, canned goods, an opener and utensils. That should be enough for now," said Cody

After the children had partially filled their sacks, they placed them in their closets.

The next afternoon the children finished loading their sacks. Cody turned to Lela. "We'll go into the forest tomorrow to find the boy."

Lela's eyes widened and she gasped and her mouth flew open. "Now I'm getting scared, Cody, should we tell Mommy and Daddy first?" she asked.

Cody whirled around facing Lela with anger in his eyes and glared at his sister. "Lela, you just said yesterday he might starve or some animal might kill him. I can't do this alone. Mom and Dad wouldn't let us go into the forest, and you know it." Flustered, Cody picked up his sack and hurled it onto the bed then turned to Lela with his hands on his hips.

"Okay, okay, I get the drift, I'll go," shrieked Lela.

At dinner that evening, Cody questioned his father. "Dad, if you thought someone was in trouble, even though you didn't know him, would you help him?"

"Of course I would, unless he was doing something wrong. You should always help someone in need or if they're sick."

"That's very true, said Robin. But you have to be cautious. Some people will take advantage of children. You have to use good judgment."

"But what if it's somewhere that's dangerous, would you still help?" asked Lela.

"It wouldn't make any difference if it's a matter of life or death. Once in a while, you have to take chances. That's part of life," said Bob.

Cody and Lela looked at each other. Their question had been answered.

4

A New Home for Elendeth

The boy ran swiftly and silently through the heavily wooded forest. Branches of trees and thickets clawed at his face and tugged at his clothes but he kept moving until he plunged waist-high into a water hole. He sucked in air as his breath burned in his lungs. Glancing around, he looked for an easy exit and pushed his way forward. He shivered and shuddered from the cold wishing he'd never stowed away in Santa's bag of toys. He spotted a low place, and headed toward it squishing his way up the soggy bank. Once out, he slowed to a walk but an icy wetness clung to his frail body, so he sped up his stride to stay warmer. Panicked, he was driven until he collapsed.

Jake, a tall unkempt, crippled man of forty with an evil past, stumbled upon the boy while searching for fallen limbs for his fireplace. He set his wood down, picked the boy up and carried him to his shack on the other side of the forest. He removed his wet clothes and dressed him in one of his old shirts. He put him to bed in a room across the hall from his then hung the clothes out to dry.

The next morning, the boy awoke and found himself dressed in a man's shirt and in a strange house. He left his room and was frightened by a gruff voice.

"Well, I see you're among the living," said Jake.

"Where am I? How did I get here? Where are my clothes?" asked the boy.

"I found you passed out in the forest, cold and wet. I brought you here and hung your clothes out to dry on the clothesline," said Jake.

"I-I don't remember anything."

"Don't matter, what's your name, boy?"

"Elendeth."

"Where are you from?"

"The North Pole, Santa's Village."

Jake broke into laughter. "Yeah, and I'm from Fairyland. That's gotta be the biggest story told this side of the Mississippi."

Elendeth looked at Jake square in the eyes with his jaw tightened. "It's the truth, I don't lie."

"All right, if that's the way you want it. Do you have a place to stay?" asked Jake.

"No," said Elendeth quietly.

"You can stay here, if you want, as long as you earn your keep. It won't be easy though."

"Yes, sir," said Elendeth, thankful that he would have a place to stay.

"You'll be hunting and fishing to put food on the table and hauling wood for the fireplace."

"I can handle that," said Elendeth.

"Above all, I don't take to cry babies or sniveling and upstairs is off-limits."

"Is that all, sir?" asked Elendeth.

"Yeah, at least for now," said Jake.

Elendeth turned and stepped outside to gather his clothes. He reached into his pants pocket and pulled out a glass-encased mustard seed. He rubbed it lovingly and clasped it tightly in his hand against his chest. "Thanks, Santa, I'll need this more now than ever." He returned it to his pocket and went inside to dress.

Early the next morning the cool winds howled. Elendeth took a gun and a fishing pole, and headed into the woods. He found the pond described by Jake but the weather turned ugly. A leaden sky with shifting clouds hung over the forest. The rain began and pounded Elendeth's slim body. He rushed for cover under a nearby tree. Lightning sizzled and thunder burst like bombs overhead and shook the ground beneath him.

After the storm, Elendeth returned to the pond to fish. He looked toward the sky. A rainbow arched majestically over the forest. He saw it as a promise and calm came over him.

When Elendeth had found enough food for supper, he had just started home when a blackbird swooshed down and plucked his hat off his head. "You thieving little rascal, come back here with my hat. If I hadn't forgotten my magic wand, I'd zap your fine-feathered little fanny." He thrust his fist into the air in anger and watched the bird fly away. Soon, the bird dropped his hat and Elendeth rushed to pick it up.

Once at home, Elendeth entered the shack. Jake was poking the fire and turned around. "That's enough for me, what are you going to eat?"

Elendeth scowled at Jake. "You're lucky to get this. There was a cloudburst out there. I'm soaking wet." He walked to the kitchen and threw his bounty into the sink and started toward his room to change into dry clothes.

"Hey, get your skinny little rump back here and clean them," yelled Jake. You're not through yet."

Elendeth turned and faced Jake. "That wasn't part of our deal," said Elendeth.

"Maybe not, but as long as you live under my roof, you'll do as I say. What do you want; me to do all the cooking and cleaning, too? What's got your undies in a wad? You hate your mama?"

Elendeth spun around with ripples of anger in his brow and pointed his finger at Jake. "I'm not your slave and keep my mother out of this."

"I told you it wasn't going to be easy," said Jake.

"Cooking and cleaning wasn't part of our deal. I'll keep my word, and that's it," said Elendeth as he headed toward his room.

In his room, sitting on the edge of the bed, hot tears trickled down his face and loneliness wrapped around him. This was the first time he'd been away from Santa and Mrs. Claus. He missed them and his usual surroundings terribly. He pulled the mustard seed from his pocket and closed his fingers around it tightly then went to bed without supper.

At dawn, Elendeth sneaked into the kitchen and grabbed a slice of bread. He picked up his hunting and fishing gear and left the house.

While at the pond, the same blackbird darted down and took his hat again. "You little beast, what do you see in my hat. I'd love to roast that little fanny of yours." Again, the blackbird dropped his hat and Elendeth ran to pick it up As he wandered through the woods hunting; he picked up fallen branches and stacked them on the forest floor to gather later.

5

The Search

After school, the bus pulled to a stop in front of the Smith home. Cody and Lela jumped off and streaked to the house. Cody unlocked the door and they scrambled upstairs. Cody tucked the ax and the can of wasp spray into his waistband. They pulled their sacks from the closet and scurried downstairs and out the door making their way toward the forest.

"This way, Lela, he went in here."

The dappled sun shone down on the children as they raced down a well-worn path. Cody spotted a murky pond and by-passed it. He headed in a different direction and into a denser part of the woods. He followed a beaten-down trail that was probably trampled by some large beast.

Lela stayed close behind her brother. "I'll start tying yarn on trees, Cody. How many trees should I skip?"

"Tie them on every sixth tree and on the longest limb."

As they entered deeper into the forest, Cody heard a growl. He stopped and looked around and spotted a coyote racing toward them. "Lela, climb a tree, hurry!" yelled Cody.

Frightened, Lela looked around and spotted an old oak with low branches. She ran to it, set her sack on the ground and began climbing. Once safe, she hollered at Cody. "Be careful, Cody, please be careful." She covered her eyes with one hand, afraid to watch.

The coyote lunged at Cody. He struck it with his ax. It yelped but came at him again and knocked him to the ground. Cody grabbed the wasp spray from his waistband and aimed it at the coyote. A jet of vapor filled its eyes. It howled and turned away weaving back and forth bumping into trees as he scrambled to get away. Cody got up and called to Lela.

"You can come down now, little sis, he's gone." Lela ran to Cody. He put his arm around her to comfort her.

Lela glanced up at Cody. "When can we start calling the boy?" she asked.

"Now is as good a time as any." Cody called out. "Boy, boy, can you hear me?"

Lela mocked her brother. "Where are you boy, can you hear us?" They trek deeper into the forest. Lela continued to tie yarn onto limbs of trees.

Elendeth had just finished stacking a pile of limbs when he heard voices. He froze in place and listened.

"Boy, where are you?" called Cody. "We've brought supplies for you. Please come out and be our friend."

Elendeth inched forward and saw the two children he'd seen Christmas morning. His heart raced excitedly. After a quick thought, Elendeth sprinted out in front of them. Startled, the children turned to run.

"No, no, don't go. I want to be your friend too. What are your names?" asked Elendeth.

The children turned back facing Elendeth. "I-I'm Cody and this is my sister, Lela. We are the ones that chased you Christmas morning."

"Yes, I recognize you."

"Why did you run away?" asked Lela.

"You were strangers in a strange land," said Elendeth.

"What do you mean?" asked Lela.

"I'm from the North Pole."

"You mean from where Santa lives?" asked Lela.

"Yep the land of the midnight sun, I'm Santa's wand elf."

"Santa's wand elf, are you spoofing us?" asked Cody.

Elendeth laughed. "No, I'm not kidding you. I am one of Santa's elves. My name is Elendeth, but you may call me Elen."

"Okay, Elen, we brought some supplies you might need. The clothes may not fit, but they'll keep you warm," said Cody.

"Yeah, and we brought food for you too," said Lela.

"Thank you. You're very kind and thoughtful," said Elen.

"Where are you staying?" asked Cody.

"A man called Jake found me and took me to his old shack on the other side of the forest. Do you know him?"

"No, I've never heard of him," said Cody.

"I haven't either," chimed Lela.

They sat on the ground to chat. Lela glanced at Elen and became aware of his funny-looking clothes but was awestruck by his dancing deep-blue eyes. Cody noticed his slightly pointed ears and friendly smile.

"Why were you in our house Christmas morning?" asked Lela.

"How old are you?" asked Cody.

"How did you get here?" asked Lela.

Elen laughed. "Whoa, slow down. I stowed away in Santa's bag of toys and slipped down the chimney with him. I had gone upstairs to peek in at you but by the time I went back downstairs, Santa was gone. As far as my age, I'm twelve years old in the elf world but our years are much longer than yours. I'll get much older as time passes, but will always look the same, since I have everlasting life; the same as all the other elves."

"Holy cow, how awesome," said Cody.

"I wish we could live forever," said Lela.

Elen winked at them. "It has it's drawback at times, believe me," he said winking again. They continued their conversation, each one learning about the other and about the place where they live.

After what seemed like a few hours, Cody looked at his watch. "Oh, gosh, we have to get home. It's almost time for Mom and Dad to be there."

"I'll walk you to the edge of the forest," said Elen. "I'm so happy you came into the forest to find me."

At the edge of the forest, Lela handed Elen the ball of yarn and scissors. "Here Elen, take these," she said. "You may need them to tie on trees to find your way around in the forest."

Cody turned the ax and the can of wasp spray over to him too. "You may need these for your protection also. The spray works great if you hit your attacker in the eyes."

They continued tromping to the edge of the forest. "You'll come back to see me, won't you?" asked Elen.

"Oh, yes, we'll come again. You are our friend now," said Cody.

Elen watched the children as they ran across the lawn and into the house. He turned back and jumped into the air. "Yahoo, friends, I have friends!" He turned cartwheels all the way back to his gun and fishing rod and the sacks the children had given him.

The children heard him holler and looked at each other and smiled.

After Elen arrived at his destination, he picked up the sacks and placed them in a crotch of a tree then tucked the can of spray into his waistband. He picked up his rifle and began hunting for rabbits or squirrels for dinner. He heard a rustle in the thickets nearby and a stab of panic overcame him. He froze. A chill rippled through him and his heart thumped wildly when he saw a huge black bear lumbering toward him. Terrified, he dropped his gun and sacks and scrambled to the nearest tree and began to climb. He shimmied up the trunk but the bear stayed at his heels climbing the tree after him. The bear reached out and clawed at Elen's foot, ripping off one of his shoes. "Ouch! Go away; get out of here!" yelled Elen as he kicked at the bear. He climbed faster and escaped to the end of a strong branch hanging on for life. The bear started out toward him. Elen reached for the can of spray in his belt and pushed the button. The bear let out a roar of pain when the mist filled his eyes. He lost his balance and fell breaking branches on his way down. Elen watched in horror as the bear got up and hobbled away. *Whew, that was a close call, he thought.*

Elen climbed down the tree and slipped into his shoe. He limped away and managed to shoot two rabbits. He shuffled to the pond and retrieved two fish he had caught earlier, and grabbed the sacks the children and brought. With a heavy load, he headed home. Before he entered the house Elen crept to his window and placed the sacks below it, then went around to the front door and entered the shack.

"What took you so long?" asked Jake. "I'm as hungry as a horse."

"Why couldn't you whip up something for yourself? It takes time to hunt and fish, they don't just fly into my arms." Elen took his prey to the kitchen and dumped them into the sink.

"Don't be a wise guy or I'll throw you out on your pointed ears," yelled Jake.

"That suits me fine Jake, I wondered how long it would take you to bad mouth my ears."

"You are one ungrateful pup," shouted Jake.

"Well, you know what they say, Jake, it takes one to know one."

Jake turned beet red with anger. He jumped up from his chair and floored Elen. When Elen got up, he turned to Jake. "Your supper is in the sink. Eat it as is or cook it; it's your choice.

Elen went to the bathroom and doctored his foot then went to his room. He opened the window and dragged the sacks inside, placing them in the closet. He was still shaken by his ordeal with the bear, and wasn't hungry, so he went to bed

6

A Welcomed Discovery

The following day Elendeth arose before dawn and browsed through the sacks the children had given him. He found peanut butter and honey sandwiches and ate one before leaving the shack empty handed.

The sun had risen in a brilliant fiery blaze that was drifting through the trees. He wandered through the forest admiring the tall trees. Cobwebs stretched from tree to tree with woven silky threads beaded with jeweled drops of dew.

He stopped at a crescent-shaped pond with crystal-clear water and sat down to rest his feet. He watched water bugs create clusters of circles as they glided across the water. A tiny frog jumped onto his lap. He smiled and lifted it off, setting it on the ground, then continued on.

After a brief time, Elen heard a yipping not far off the path. He edged over to a thicket and spotted a baby coyote. "Hey, little fella, where's your mama?" Elendeth looked around and saw nothing. "You'll starve if I leave you here. I guess you'd better come with me." He picked the pup up cradling him in his arms. The pup rose up and licked him in the face. Elen smiled, pet him, and moved on.

A driving force pushed Elen deeper into the forest. Something blue caught his eye as it dashed in front of him. Curious, he ambled to an opening in the thicket. His eyes widened and his mouth flew open. "A reindeer, a blue reindeer,"

The reindeer looked up at Elen. "Of course I'm a reindeer and, yes, I'm blue."

"Y-You can talk? All the reindeer I know are brown and they can't talk."

"Brown is an ugly color. Yes, I can talk."

"My name is Elendeth, but you may call me Elen. What's your name?"

"Pereguinnes, but that's such an odd name to remember, you may call me Pere."

Elen spotted an almost perfect white star on Pere's forehead. He ambled toward him. "May I feel your beautiful coat, Pere? It looks so soft."

"Sure, no problem."

Elen sauntered over and stroked his coat of blue. When he touched the star on Pere's forehead, a burst of electricity surged through his body knocking him backwards and onto the ground. The pup yelped and wiggled loose. Elen sat up. "Whoa, what a shocker that was. What the devil happened?" asked Elen.

Pere snickered. "Sorry, I forgot to mention the power of the star on my forehead, it's magical."

"Magic, huh? Sure wish I had some of it. I forgot my wand at Santa's house." Elen bent down and picked the pup up.

"Where did the pup come from?"

"I found him forsaken before I met you," said Elen. "My lucky day I guess."

"He has a beautiful silver sheen to his hair."

"He does have a pretty color, doesn't he? Hey, I have to hunt for a while then head back home. Would you like to tag along?"

"I'd love to. It beats being alone all day with no one to talk to. Do you live around here?"

"I'm living on the other side of the forest. I'm in the forest every day looking for food. Why don't we meet up; that is, if you'd like to."

"That would be great and real nice to have a friend," said Pere.

Elen smiled gratefully for having company. "I'd like that, too. We can visit while I hunt and fish."

While rambling through the forest, Elen told Pere his story. "I wound up here when I stowed away in Santa's bag of toys. It had been my dream to see the rest of the world, but it's been a nightmare instead. I was a real knot-head to do something stupid like that. I had gone upstairs on one of Santa's stops to peek in at the children but when I went back down, Santa had left. Now I have to figure out how to get back home."

"I reckon you asked for trouble all right. It seems that we're in the same boat; so to speak," said Pere.

"You're right about that but I don't like it here, and eventually, I have to return home; I have no choice."

"Why do you say that?" asked Pere.

"It's a matter of life or death."

"Life or death?" asked Pere.

"Yeah, either I stay here and die or go home and live forever. It's complicated."

"I'm not sure I understand your reasoning, but I'll take your word for it. I didn't like it here either but I've learned to love the peace. You will too, Elen, it's just a matter of time."

"Why do you think we're in the same boat, Pere?"

"The reason I said that is I'm from a different planet and you're from the Arctic."

"You are? What planet is that?" asked Elen.

"Sedna."

"Wow, I guess we do have a lot in common," said Elen.

Once Elen had his share of game, they headed toward the shack. Pere walked with him half way, then left his company promising to see him tomorrow.

When Elen arrived home, Jake was drunk. "Well, if it isn't the little vagabond. Get that mangy mutt out of my house," Jake screamed.

"I prefer to be called Elen. He's a pup, Jake. He needs to be taken care of."

"Not on my watch and not in my house."

"I'll keep him in my room. He won't be bothersome."

"I said NO! Get that flea-bitten mutt out NOW," hollered Jake or I'll take a hammer to his head."

Elen looked at Jake with hate in his eyes. "You really would, wouldn't you? Do you always put someone down, human or animal?" questioned Elen. "I do a lot for you, Jake, you could at least show some respect and let me keep the pup inside."

Jake ran over and picked up a broom. "No respect you say? I said NO. You aren't keeping him in my house. He headed toward Elen and the pup. "If you wouldn't take so much time finding dinner, maybe things would be different. Jake paused momentarily; by the way, where is dinner?"

"I didn't work today. I needed a break."

"A break? A break? I'll give you a break. I'll break your fool neck along with the pups." Jake started toward Elen with the broom in the air.

Elen's face reddened with anger but he stood his ground and stepped forward. "I'm not afraid of you, Jake, and I don't take orders from you. You're a heartless and selfish old man."

"You're getting smart-mouthed, sonny-boy, better watch your back."

Elen stormed to Jake. "Is that a threat?"

"It could be," said Jake.

Elen turned away not wanting to create a problem. "You're impossible," he said and stomped out the door. Outside, he looked for a safe place to keep the pup. He found an old orange crate and set it under his window. "This will do for now but keep it low when you yelp. We don't need someone hitting you over the head with a hammer."

Elen went back into the house and to his room. He dragged the sacks out of the closet and rummaged through them. He found sandwiches the children had left for him. He opened the window and fed the pup. He went to the kitchen for a cup of water and back to his room. He set the cup of water in the crate for the pup.

After the pup was cared for, Elen sat on the edge of the bed and ate. He took the glass-encased mustard seed out of his pocket and looked at it sadly. *What have I done, Santa? You and Mrs. Claus didn't deserve this. I'm sorry, Santa, I'm so very sorry.* Elen clasped the mustard seed tightly then put it back in his pocket; then his thoughts turned to Pere. He was anxious to see him again.

At dawn, Elen grabbed the pup and left the house early with his hunting and fishing gear. He found Pere at the brook sipping water. "Good morning, Pere. Hope your night went better than mine."

Pere looked up at Elen. "Why do you say that?"

"When you think things couldn't get any worse; they get far worse."

"I'm sorry to hear that, Elen. How about a stroll to the pond? I'll watch, and we'll chat while you fish."

"Sure thing," said Elen downhearted. He set the pup down.

Without warning, the blackbird darted down and yanked Elen's hat off his head again. "Dagnabit, bring my hat back you rotten bird. If I had my magic wand, you wouldn't have any feathers left in that fine feathered little rump of yours."

Pere chuckled. "It looks like you have a friend."

Elen looked at Pere with surprise. "A friend? Him a friend? Never! I have enough trouble at home. I don't need any more."

"I find that hard to believe, Elen. You befriended me and a coyote pup, why not a bird? One day you may discover he is a friend and perhaps one of your best." Pere chuckled again. "You know, Elen, it's been said that when you're teased, you are liked; otherwise you're not."

"Well, I'm not in any mood to make a friend and especially with a bratty bird." Elen was ranting and raving when he spotted him. He pointed his finger at him. "I'll get you one day, just you wait and see." A spark of lightning flew from the tip of Elen's finger. KA-BLAM! It hit the bird's fanny and feathers floated down to the forest floor.

"Caw, caw, caw," cried the bird and flew away.

When the pup saw the sparks fly, he yipped and ran under Elen with his tail tucked between his legs. Elen and Pere looked down at him and bellowed with laughter. The pup was shaking with fright. Elen knelt down and picked him up. "Holy moly, did you see that Pere? Did that come from me? How did that happen?"

Pere snickered. "You received magic when you touched the star on my forehead."

"I did? I really did? All right, that's amazing. You've made me whole again, Pere, and you've made my day. I don't think anything could go wrong the rest of the afternoon. Thank you, Pere."

"You are more than welcome, my friend."

Elen looked at the pup in his arms. "You're okay little one, you'll have to get used to seeing the sparks fly, that's part of me now; it's magic." Elen's chest swelled with pride.

While Elen fished, the pup sat at his side. His mind turned to Jake, and he became sullen; Pere noticed the change in Elen. "What's wrong, friend?" asked Pere.

"It's Jake. He's such a pain. I hunt, I fish, I collect firewood. I try to please him, mind you. He warned me it was not going to be easy, and it surely isn't. Just trying to get along with him is difficult."

"You'll figure things out one day" said Pere. Things are bound to get better for you."

"I've made a real mess for myself. I have no friends and no way to get home."

"I'm your friend and I happen to like you," said Pere.

Elen looked at Pere with surprise. "Thanks, Pere, you just made my day again. That means a lot to me."

"You must have other friends, too. I hear them calling your name."

Elen's face lit up. "All right, come on, let's go. I want you to meet them." Elen grabbed the pup.

"Climb on board, friend, we'll get there faster." Elen hopped on holding the pup tightly.

"Hang on, we're going up," hollered Pere.

Elen grabbed hold of Pere's antlers not anticipating what Pere meant. Soon he felt them lifting off the ground. Elen looked down. "Oh, oh, oh, you can fly?"

"Better believe it, friend, we're in the air."

"Holy guacamole! We can fly; wooohoooooo!"

While they were airborne, Elen looked out over the trees. He spotted a man on a nearby road watching them with his mouth wide open in disbelief.

Soon Pere lowered himself to the ground and trotted to the edge of the forest. The children's eye's popped open and their jaws dropped. They stared in wonder and disbelief.

"A blue reindeer he's beautiful," cried Lela.

"He sure is a beauty," said Cody. What's his name, Elen?"

"It's Pere. Hop on; we'll hitch a ride to the brook." Elen helped the children on and handed the pup to Cody then jumped onto Pere's rump.

"Where did you get the coyote, Elen?" asked Cody.

"Why is Pere blue?" asked Lela.

"One question at a time, okay? It's a long story, I'll tell you at the brook," said Elen.

"They're nice, I like them both," said Cody.

"I love them," said Lela.

When they arrived at the brook they found a fallen log and a tree stump to sit on.

"So you want to hear a story, huh?" asked Elen.

"Yes," the children chided at the same time with excitement.

"Well, Elen said, I met Pere in the forest one day while I was wandering. A streak of blue flashed in a path ahead of me. I was curious as to what it was, so I stopped at the thicket he ran into, and there he was broader than daylight and blue as the sky."

"Why is he blue?" asked Lela.

"That's a question I can't answer. I don't know, Princess," said Elen.

"Where did you get the coyote pup?" asked Cody.

"I found him abandoned in the woods before I found Pere."

"They're going to be part of our family now, aren't they Elen?" asked Cody.

"They surely are."

"I love them, Elen," said Lela.

"Speaking of family, I'd like to come over and meet your parents. When would be a good day?"

"Oh, uh, oh, I guess Saturday. That would be good because they aren't working."

"B-But Cody," cried Lela

"Shush, Lela."

"But...

Cody turned and gave Lela a knock-it-off-look so she sat back and said nothing more.

7

The Confession

That night Cody lightly tapped on Lela's door and stepped inside. He sat down on the side of her bed. Lela looked up and saw his troubled face.

"What's wrong, Cody?"

"It's everything. We've been pulling the wool over Mom and Dad's eyes far too long, Lela. Now that Elen and Pere are coming on Saturday, we have no choice but to tell them. We'll do it tonight at supper," said Cody.

Lela's temper flared up. "NO, not yet, why did you have to open your big mouth and tell them they could come over? We'll be in a heap of trouble and they probably won't let us see them anymore. Sometimes I hate you, Cody."

Cody lowered his eyes then looked up at her. "Lela, I knew it was wrong, and you knew it too. There will be a big weight lifted off my shoulders when we tell them. There is no doubt that we won't be punished, we both knew that. You know Dad and how strict he is. He will punish us, but for how long I don't know, but he would never deny us ever seeing them again. We were wrong, now we have to face up to it and accept our punishment."

"But I'm scared, Cody," Lela said as tears started rolling down her cheeks. "I want to see them every day. I love them."

"I love them too, but honesty is the best policy, little sis. Not sneaking behind their backs and doing things we know we shouldn't be doing. We will lose their trust in us. Do you want that to happen?"

"No," said Lela wiping her eyes.

"Remember what they said about helping someone in need, even if it's a dangerous place? That's exactly what we did. We have to believe in them."

"I remember, but I'm still scared, Cody."

"I know little sis, I'm a bit scared myself, but we'll get through this together and try to do our best the next time, okay?"

"Okay, I guess, but I don't like it."

When the children were called to dinner, Cody looked at Lela and swallowed then he proceeded to confess. "Dad, Mom, we have a confession to make. Lela and I have been going into the forest to find a boy we saw in our house on Christmas morning. We went in to find him then we started taking food and clothes to him."

"YOU DID WHAT?" screamed Bob.

"I'm sorry Dad, but he needed help."

"I'm sorry too, Mommy and Daddy but we were afraid a mean animal might get him," cried Lela.

Bob looked at Lela then slammed his fork down on the table with brute force. The children's eyes popped wide open and they jumped back in their chair. "And what made you think that mean animal wouldn't get you?" yelled Bob.

Tears started rolling down Lela's cheeks.

Robin reached over and patted Bob's arm. "Well, was he okay when you found him?" asked Robin.

"Yes Mom. He told us a man found him and took him to his place. He said he has to hunt and fish every day to put food on the table in exchange for room and board."

"And he has to collect wood for his fireplace too," said Lela.

"What in the world was he doing in our house? How did he get in? Are we not safe in our own home anymore?" yelled Bob again.

"He's Santa's wand elf, Dad," said Cody. "He stowed away in Santa's sack of toys."

"Yeah, and he came down the chimney with Santa," said Lela excitedly.

"He went upstairs to see us but by the time he went downstairs, Santa was gone," said Cody.

Bob shook his head. "Oh, yes, that explains it all. And I saw a horse in a pink tutu dancing down the stairs on Christmas morning too. Do you really expect us to believe that hogwash?"

Bob was angry. Robin reached over and patted him on his arm again. "Calm down, Bob. The children are innocent until proven guilty. Can we meet him?" asked Robin.

"Yes," they'll be here Saturday afternoon," said Cody.

"They?" asked Bob

"Yes, Daddy, he has a blue reindeer," chimed Lela excitedly.

'The reindeer's name is Pere," said Cody.

"And he can fly Daddy, like Santa's reindeer," cried Lela.

Bob threw his arms into the air. "You can't possibly believe what you expect us to believe," he shouted.

"But it's true, Daddy, honest it is," said Lela fidgeting in her chair.

"Well, we'll wait until tomorrow to meet them," said Robin.

Bob sighed. "All right, we'll wait before we decide on your punishment for disobeying."

"Okay, Dad. That sounds fair. We knew we were doing wrong," admitted Cody.

Saturday afternoon Cody and Lela were waiting in the back yard for Elen and Pere to arrive. When they flew in, Cody ran to them. "Elen, I told Mom and Dad about you, but I don't think they believed me."

Elen placed his hand on Cody's shoulder. "Don't fret; we'll see what happens when we meet."

A few minutes later Bob and Robin stepped onto the back porch. Their mouth flew open in disbelief.

Elen strolled up to them and thrust his hand out to Bob for a handshake. "Hello, I'm Elen. I've had a desire to meet you ever since I met your delightful children."

Bob and Robin stood spellbound and speechless but Bob reached out to return Elen's handshake.

Cody stepped up. "Dad, Mom, these are our forest friends, Elen and Pere. The coyote belongs to Elen."

Bob and Robin stood dumbfounded, and in shock.

Elen broke the silence. "I asked Cody if we could come over to meet you. He was nice enough to agree. I hope you don't mind."

Bob's spell was broken. "Oh, uh no, no, not at all, Elen. We're very anxious to hear more about you and Pere. It must be quite a story."

"Come on in, Elen, I'll start supper," said Robin. "Cody, run out and fetch water and grain for Pere."

Elen set the coyote down. "You stay here with Pere, little one. Don't be wandering off."

Cody and Lela ran to the barn for grain and filled a bucket with water. They rushed back and placed it in front of Pere then ran into the house not wanting to miss a moment with Elen. They sat on each side of him on the couch.

Bob sat back in his overstuffed chair. "Tell us more about yourself, Elen. What are your plans now that you're here?"

"And tell us about Santa, too," piped Lela.

"I'm sure the children have told you how I got here," said Elen.

"Yes, they have," said Bob.

"I've lived with Santa and Mrs. Claus all my life. They have been very compassionate and supportive of me. Santa is a very kind and gentle man with a heart as big as the moon. He loves all little children no matter their race or color. I was blessed to be raised by him."

"Where are your parents, Elen?" asked Cody.

"I don't know. I was left on Santa's doorstep after I was born."

Lela gasped. "Oh, no."

"Why would they do that?" asked Cody. "I can't imagine living without my parents."

"Well, the way I see it, when life throws you oranges, you make lemonade. I never regretted being raised by Santa."

Lela giggled. "You mean lemons, Elen? You can't make lemonade with oranges."

Elen looked at Lela and winked. "Yes Princess, lemons."

"I don't know why I was left on Santa's doorstep but I know it was a good thing. If I had been raised in the Elf Kingdom, I wouldn't have had freedom as I did with Santa and Mrs. Claus."

"Do all the other elves live in the Kingdom?" asked Lela.

"Yes, they do. They walk to work every day to Santa's toy shop from October through December."

"Oh, like the dwarfs in the Snow White movie?" asked Lela. She sat by Elen listening and was enchanted with his stories of how he was raised.

Elen smiled. "Yes, but the dwarfs were free, unlike the elves."

"What did you do in Santa's workshop, Elen?" asked Cody.

"I made hundreds of music boxes every year among other toys."

"What are your plans for the future, Elen," asked Bob.

"I have no plans other than finding a way home."

"No, Elen! I want you to stay here," shouted Lela.

Elen's face lit up with a broad smile as he looked at Lela.

"Supper is ready," called Robin. "Come and get it!"

Cody jumped up. "Come on, Elen, let's eat."

Lela grabbed Elen by the hand and led him to the kitchen.

The children chose to sit on each side of Elen. After seated, the family joined hands. Lela and Cody quickly grabbed one of Elen's hands and bowed their heads in prayer before eating. Elen followed.

After dinner, Elen arose from the table. "The dinner was delicious, Ms. Robin. I haven't had a home-cooked meal since I left home. I appreciate your hospitality."

"Stay a while Elen. Let's mosey over to the family room and chat a little more," said Bob.

"Sounds good," said Elen.

After settling in the family room, Bob began asking Elen more questions. "You've never met your parents, you say, Elen?"

"No, I haven't. Who knows, maybe it was for the best," said Elen.

"The reason I asked is you are quite tall for an elf, aren't you?"

"Yes, I am taller than most."

"How did you fit into Santa's bag of toys?" asked Lela.

Elen winked at Lela and chuckled. "I found his magic dust quite by accident."

"You did?" Lela's eyes widened and she gulped. "How?" she asked.

"I was in Santa's office one day and I wasn't supposed to be there. I heard him coming so I climbed the ladder to the top of a vat. I didn't know the lid was open and I fell in. It was Santa's magic dust. I had a hard time getting out because it shrunk me down to almost nothing. It was a good thing there was a long handled ladle in there or I would never have gotten out. After I finally made it out, I grabbed a handful of his magic dust and hid it in my room until I was ready to climb into his sack on Christmas Eve. Once the dust wore off, I returned to my normal size." Elen glanced at Cody and Lela. "Children can be devious little devils at times, can't they?" said Elen, as he winked at them.

Bob chortled. "You can say that again, Elen."

The children were all ears as they listened to Elen. They laughed merrily when he finished telling of his adventure.

Elen looked at Bob. "What do you and Ms. Robin do for a living, Bob?"

"We're both teachers. I work at the local college and Robin is a grammar school teacher."

"Now I understand why the children are sharp little whipper-snappers," said Elen smiling.

After a pleasing and delightful evening, Elen stood. "I must go now. It has been a pleasure meeting you both and a delightful visit. He turned to Ms. Robin and nodded his head. "You are an excellent cook, Ms. Robin. I enjoyed the meal very much, thank you. I hope we'll be seeing a lot of each other."

"That we will," said Bob. "It has been a very special visit for us too, Elen."

"It surely was an unexpected, and an exciting visit from one of Santa's people," said Robin. We will cherish the memory always."

Elen grabbed his hat, placed it on his head, then tipped it and bowed. "I thank you both for your generosity." He left after the goodbyes.

The children became sullen after Elen left. Bob looked down at them. "I have mixed emotions. I'm proud of you for helping someone in need, however, you should have come to us and we could have worked things out together. As it is now, you must be punished for disobeying."

"We both knew we would be in trouble, Dad, and we accept it," said Cody. "May I ask a question?"

"Sure, what is it, son?" asked Bob

"What did you think of Elen?" asked Cody.

"He is a very fine and exceptional young man. The two of you made a brilliant choice by choosing him for a friend," said Bob.

"Yes, I agree, and what a hoot to see a blue reindeer," said Robin.

The children giggled after hearing their mother's remark. Cody was relieved. "Thanks Mom and Dad."

"I'm sorry I was cross with you but rules are rules and are not to be broken," said Bob. Your punishment will be that you will not see Elen or Pere for one week, no exceptions."

Lela burst into tears and the size of raindrops rolled down her cheeks spilling onto her clothing. "But, Daddy, that's a long time."

Bob looked at her. "It may seem to be a long time to you because you are still a child, but you'll learn a valuable lesson, won't you Lela?"

"Yes Daddy."

The next day Bob saddled Tivvy and rode into the forest to find Elen. With Cody's directions, he found him at the brook with Pere.

Elen glanced up when Bob rode in. "Hi Bob, what brings you into the forest?"

"I came to let you know the children are on restriction for coming into the forest without permission. They won't be allowed to see you or Pere for a week."

"Okay, I understand, Bob. I'll miss seeing them but I'm sure it'll be a good lesson. Thanks for the heads up."

"Sure. We'll see you at the end of the week," said Bob and turned to leave.

Lela moped every day after their punishment was handed down. She thought of them day and night and couldn't wait to see them again. She went into the living room and flipped on the television set and flopped down on an over-sized beanbag. Tears of sadness gushed down her cheeks out of loneliness. *How am I going to last a whole week, she thought. I knew we should have asked Mommy and Daddy first.*

Elen lay awake that night thinking about many things. He had to get away from Jake, but where would he go? If he lived in the forest, where would he sleep? What would he eat? How can I get back home? A sudden idea came to mind that would solve everything. He would talk to Pere about it tomorrow. He rolled over and went to sleep.

When Elen awoke the next morning, he was anxious to see Pere. He grabbed the pup and his gear and took off. Pere was grazing when he found him. "Pere, I had a great idea during the night."

Pere raised his head. "Yeah, what's that, Elen?"

"You can fly so you could take me back home so how about it, Pere?"

"Uh, uh, I may be able to fly but I'm not flying you to the North Pole. It's too far, and too cold."

"But, Pere…."

"No, I'm not going. You'll get used to it and love it here, just as I have."

"But, I owe Santa."

"Owe Santa for what, Elen, for raising you? I'm sure Santa enjoyed every minute with you and didn't expect anything more than that pleasure. It's plain and simple Elen, you're acting like a wimpy little kid."

Elen sat down and began to sulk. *No matter what I say or do, Pere is not going to take me home, thought Elen.*

"Not going to do you any good to sulk, my friend, I still won't go. Be happy you're here and in good health with good friends. It'll work out much better for you," said Pere.

"You don't understand, Pere."

"I understand all right. We were placed here for a reason. Mine is to find happiness. Not sure about you, but everything happens for a cause. Be patient and you'll find out what that reason is."

Elen picked up his pole and wandered to the pond to fish. The pup sat quietly alongside of him. "Well, I don't know about you, little one, but I guess I'm doomed to stay here, like it or not. That's what I get for stowing away, huh girl?"

The pup looked up at Elen then licked his hand as if to say; "It's okay at least we'll be together."

After Pere's rejection, Elen was bombed out. It had not been the perfect day he had hoped for. Days passed, and things got worse between Elen and Jake.

One night Elen was awakened by someone calling his name. He thought it was a dream but he lay there and listened. Soon, he heard his name being called again. The call came from outside. He went to the window and opened it.

"It's about time. I'm soaked to the skin. I'll catch my death of pneumonia," said the pup.

Elen looked wide-eyed at the pup. "Oh no, not you too!" Elen stood dumbfounded.

"Don't just stand there like a dork, aren't you going to invite me in?" asked the pup.

"Oh, yes, of course." Elen bent over the window sill and took him out of the crate. He went to the closet for a shirt and wiped him dry. "When did you lean to talk?" whispered Elen.

"I listened, I saw, and I copied," said the pup.

"You little wooly burger, you are one sharp cookie. You must have been blessed with magic at the same time I was. We'll have to be very quiet or we'll both be hit over the head with a hammer," said Elen.

"I'd like to bury a hatchet in his head," said the pup, and my name isn't wooly burger or cookie; it's Pearl, and why can't you people tell a girl from a boy?"

"Shh, shh, we don't want to wake him. Climb into bed so you can warm up." The pup jumped onto the bed and ducked under the covers.

Elen was in good spirits the next day when he went into the forest. "Good morning, Pere."

Pere looked up from grazing. "What makes you so happy this morning?"

"Guess what?" asked Elen.

"What's up your sleeve this time, friend?"

"You're not going to believe this, Pere, but the pup can talk and, by the way, she told me her name is Pearl."

"A talking coyote? That's nonsense."

"It's true, Pere"

Pere turned to Pearl. "Okay, talk to me little missy. Say something Pearl." Pere waited but there was no response. He looked at Elen. "Uh huh, just as I thought, Elen, the jigs up, you're full of crackers."

"I'm not kidding, she really can talk, maybe she's being shy," said Elen.

"Knock off your foolishness and get outta here," said Pere.

Pearl looked at Elen then at Pere. "Pere, Pere, quite contrary," said Pearl.

Pere looked at Pearl wide-eyed and started guffawing. He dropped to the ground rolling from side to side with his legs kicking in the air. When he got up, his tail was spinning in circles.

Elen cackled. "Careful, Pere, you're so wound up, you'd better hold onto that tail or you may go up like a helicopter."

"I'll be a polka-dotted donkey, said Pere. "I never thought I'd hear a coyote talk instead of howl." Pere let out a coyote's howl.

"Taint funny donkey," said Pearl looking at Pere with disgust.

Pere snickered. "I hear those wheels a-turnin' comin' round the bend. You sound like someone I know; think, think, think," said Pere.

"I know who you're talking about and you'd better knock it off, or I'll knock you off," said Pearl. Elen had to turn around to hide his smile from Pere.

After work, Elen and Pearl walked into the house and Jake was on their backs immediately.

"I told you I didn't want that mangy beast in this house" Jake picked up a broom and began hitting Pearl.

"Stop it!" yelled Elen, "You'll kill her."

"Good, then I'll take care of you," screamed Jake.

Elen glared at Jake. "You are one crotchety old man." He dropped his gear and catches on the floor and picked up Pearl and went to his room. He gathered his belongings, grabbed the sacks and walked to the door.

"Where do you think you're going?" asked Jake.

"Anywhere. Anywhere away from you."

"Who's gonna hunt, who's gonna fish? Who's gonna haul wood? Where are you gonna stay?" asked Jake.

"Beats me," said Elen as he slammed the door behind him.

8

A Forest Home

Elen wandered into the forest calling Pere's name. Soon Pere landed facing him.

"What's up?" he asked.

"Where's the best place to bed down around here?" asked Elen.

"You moving in?" asked Pere excitedly.

"Yep, can't handle being around Jake anymore."

"Good, welcome home, my friend. I've got the best place in the forest for you and the pup," said Pere. "Follow me."

Pere led them to some thickets with a deep and sturdy overhead with a space to enter and look out over the forest.

"Wow, this is perfect, thanks," Pere.

Elen and Pearl entered the hut. Elen took a blanket from one of his sacks and spread it on the ground then he rolled his jacket up for a pillow. He looked out the door and watched Pearl sniffing around to get accustomed to her new home. Soon he saw her squat. Elen laughed. "Marking your territory, huh, girl?"

That evening as Elen lay, he listened to strange sounds in the forest. He got a whiff of smoke in the air. *Most likely from a fireplace, he thought. He remembered when he and Santa sat by the fire and enjoyed a cup of hot chocolate in a silver goblet and chatted about the day. I miss you Santa, you were so right to refuse to take me with you; I WAS too immature, he thought.*

Looking out into the forest, Elen noticed the trees blocking the view of the sky and they were casting feathery shadows on the ground. *It's beautiful out here, and it's such a relief to get away from that mad man.* He reached over and patted Pearl on the head. "Good night, little one," then he called out to Pere, "Good night, Pere," and turned over and went to sleep.

Pere stayed by his hut to keep a vigilant watch over him through the night. He felt there was something special about Elen. *It must be the kindness and thoughtfulness in him, he thought. He'll be my best friend and I'll be faithful till the end.*

When Elen awoke the next morning, he called out to Pere. "Hey Pere: how about a ride into the forest? I need to find a limb to make a fishin' pole. Don't have anything else to do with the little ones still on restriction."

"Sure, hop on, Elen, no problem."

They wandered through the forest until Elen spotted a branch he liked. "Aha! Over there Pere; there's a perfect one." Elen pointed to an old oak tree. Pere wandered over to it and Elen jumped off. He took his knife from his belt and cut off the branch then removed the limbs.

"What are you going to use for string and a hook, Elen?" asked Pere.

"Got it all figured out. A vine and a safety pin oughta do the trick. As far as bait, I'm gonna use tadpoles."

"Tadpoles? Yuk, that doesn't sound too appetizing," said Pere.

Elen laughed. "I wouldn't worry, my friend, you won't be the one eating them."

Pere snickered, "I wouldn't touch them with a ten-foot pole," he said.

After Elen tied the vine to the pole, he reached into his pocket and pulled out a safety pin and attached it to the end of the vine. "Well, I reckon it's ready to catch a fish but let's stop by the hut and set up some rocks for a fire. Gotta pick up a bucket the little ones gave me too."

Once they arrived at the hut, Elen gathered rocks and cleaned an area to start a fire. He placed the rocks in a circle. Then he grabbed the bucket and said, "Let's go Pere." As they started out, Elen began singing a tune. "Ohh, a fishin' we will go, a fishin' we will go, hi-ho a fishin' hole, a fishin' we will go."

Pere laughed. "You really get into the swing of things don't you, Elen?"

"Well, I see it this way, my friend, gotta find somethin' to pass time while the children are away. It may as well be a good supper."

"Yeah, I miss those children. They're a couple of cute kids," said Pere.

The pup followed and was playfully trying to hide from Elen. She would rush into the thickets then jump out at him when he approached.

Elen laughed. "Wanna play games, huh, little one?"

When they arrived at the pond, Elen swung the bucket into the water next to the bank and brought out a bunch of tadpoles. He placed a tadpole on the hook, threw it into the water and waited. Soon, he felt something tugging at the vine. "I got a bite, I got a bite," he yelled. He pulled the line out but there was nothing on it, not even the tadpole.

"Better luck next time, Elen," said Pere.

In the meantime, the pup had jumped into the water trying to catch a fish too. Elen called out to him. "Hey, get your little fanny outta there before I give you a good zap." The pup jumped out next to Elen and shook himself.

"You little rascal, now you've gotten us all wet." Elen threw the line in again and again and failed each time to catch a fish. "Hmph, maybe they don't like tadpoles, Pere."

"So, what are you going to do?"

While Elen pondered his next move, he glanced up at a large oak. "Hey, look at the bees up there, Pere," as he pointed at the tree.

"Yeah, they probably have honey in the hole."

"Honey? I'd better check it out."

"No, Elen, I wouldn't do that if I were you."

"Why not? It's food, isn't it?"

"Yeah, but... Elen ignored Pere's warning and climbed the oak like it was a ladder. When he reached the hive he stuck his hand in the hole and felt the sticky honey and grabbed a handful. When he brought his hand out, the bees swarmed around him. Quickly, Elen slid down the tree headed for the water. He screamed all the way to the pond. "Owww, oh, ouch! Pere, help."

Pere was standing at the edge of the pond cracking up. "I warned you, you little fool. Jump in, jump in!" yelled Pere.

Elen came up licking his fingers. "Ummm, umm, umm, that sure is good."

"It might be good now, just wait a while and we'll see how good you think it was," said Pere.

Elen's thoughts turned back to the bait. He took his knife out of his pocket and started digging near the water. After a while, he pulled out a long, juicy worm. "What about this Pere?" Elen stuck the worm with the sharp point of the pin several times winding it around then tied it.

"That looks yucky, Elen."

Elen laughed and threw the vine into the water. "Whack," he caught a fish. He pulled the vine out and gazed at the fine catfish. "Look at that, Pere, just look at that. There's our supper. It sure would have been easier with a real pole, though."

"I'm sure it would have, Elen."

Elen picked up his bucket with the fish and they headed home. When they arrived, he collected small fallen limbs and stacked them in a cross-hatch fashion then struck a match to start the fire. After cleaning the fish, he speared it with a long, sturdy limb and began to cook it. He continued his effort until his dinner was a feast of juicy roasted catfish.

After eating Elen said, "Wow, that was delicious, even if I say so myself," as he rubbed his tummy. A chef-boy-ar-dee, I am, I am. We'll have to do that more often, Pere." Elen brought his thumb and finger together for an "okay" sign. They both laughed.

He offered some to Pearl. She smelled it, wrinkled her nose but ate it anyway. "It sure would be nice if it was as easy to catch a jack rabbit to roast," said Elen. "Guess we'll have to teach you how to chase jack rabbits, Pearl" said Elen laughing.

Later that evening, Elen showed Pere his swollen hand. "Golly, it hurts, Pere. What can I put on it to help the pain?"

"We can't go to the house. The children aren't allowed to see us so we'll have to substitute the medication. Grab your bucket and get some potash from the fire. Be careful about hot coals, we don't need a burn too."

Elen grabbed the bucket and set it near the fire. He used a flat piece of bark to scoop up the potash and placed it in the bucket. "What now?" asked Elen.

"You have any water?"

"Bottled water the children brought."

"Pour some over your hand then dip it in the potash," said Pere.

Elen did as Pere told him. "Whoa, that feels better all ready. Thanks, Pere, I don't think I'll ever try that stupid thing again. Next time I'll listen to your advice."

Elen started the fire up again, knowing he'd be up suffering from the stings. They stayed up late into the night talking as the fire crackled and burned sweet-scented wood.

It was early morning when they decided to turn in. Elen scraped the ground for dirt and placed it on the fire until it died out. "Thanks for your help, Pere. My hand feels much better...still hurts but it's much better; goodnight." Elen turned and went into the hut and Pearl followed.

9

A Castle in the Forest

When the week of punishment was over for the children, Cody approached his father. "Dad, may we go into the forest to see Elen and Pere today?"

"Please, Daddy?" asked Lela. "And can Elen build a tree house for us?" asked Lela.

Bob looked at the children with his hands on his hips. "Hmm," he said thinking. Well, I suppose so since you've been so good. Yes, and I think we can have Elen build it as long as it's close to him. If he'll build it, I'll buy the lumber and what will be needed."

"Hooray!" Lela yelled as she jumped up and down. "Let's go tell Elen, Cody," she yelled excitedly.

"Thanks, Dad," said Cody.

The children gathered supplies and cookies that Robin had made for Elen and ran to the barn. Cody saddled Tivvy and they rode to Elen's hut. When they arrived, they jumped down and ran to him.

"Elen, we're off restriction now," said Cody. "Dad said we can have a tree house if you'll build it for us. I sure missed you and Pere," he added.

"Yeah, and I missed you too, Elen and the tree house has to be built close to you," shouted Lela. "And Daddy said he would buy the lumber."

Elen smiled. "Of course, I'll build one, but there'll be a catch."

Cody raised his eyebrows. "A catch, what's that mean?" he asked.

"Yep, you'll have to wait until I finish it before you can see it."

"How long, Elen?" asked Lela.

"Oh, probably a month," said Elen.

"Another month? That's too long, Elen," said Lela.

"That's not fair," said Cody. "I wanted to help."

Elen shrugged his shoulders. "It's either that or no tree house," said Elen.

"Oh, okay, that's okay, Cody," said Lela.

Cody whirled around glaring at Lela. "Whatdoya mean that's okay, Lela?"

"My teacher told me I have to bring a dead egg to school," said Lela, "and it might take me a long time to find one so you can help me look."

"A dead egg?" Elen asked arching his eyebrows and scratching his head.

"I don't wanna help you find a stupid dead egg," shouted Cody.

"You are priceless, Princess. Well, Cody, Lela is right. It probably will take her a long time to find one, so maybe you should help," said Elen.

Cody looked at Elen, then back at Lela. "You sure know how to foul things up, Lela."

"What do you mean, Cody?" asked Lela.

"Nothing, its history now," said Cody as he kicked at a pine cone sending it sailing.

Elen reached over and mussed Cody's hair and winked at him.

"Cody, let's go see Pere," shouted Lela.

"I guess," said Cody. He felt, between Lela and Elen, the wind had been knocked out from under his sails. He was so disappointed he couldn't help Elen.

"Run along," said Elen, "he'll be happy to see you."

When they found Pere, Lela shouted, "Hi, Pere! We came to spend the day with you and Elen. We missed you a lot," she said.

Pere nodded his head.

"Could you give us a ride in the forest today?" asked Cody.

Pere nodded his head yes and knelt down on his front knees for them to climb on. He headed for Elen's hut. When they arrived at the hut, Cody called out. "Elen, come with us to take a ride in the forest."

Elen stepped out of the hut. "Okay, I'm ready for a big adventure," and he jumped onto Pere's rump.

Pere headed into the deepest part of the forest. The children looked from side to side watching squirrels, chipmunks and rabbits scampering about on the forest floor.

"Elen," asked Cody, "can we choose our own Christmas tree when Christmas is here?"

"Sure, I'll build a travois to haul it on."

"What's a travois?" asked Lela.

"It's like a sled that Indians used years ago to haul trees and other personal or heavy things. They even hauled their children on it," said Elen.

"Can we ride on it, too?" asked Lela.

"Sure," said Elen.

As they went deeper into the forest, the canopy of trees overhead became thicker and the forest became darker. Suddenly, Elen ordered Pere to stop. Elen listened and then saw a huge black bear lumbering toward them with thunderous growls. The children screamed.

Elen held up a hand in the halt position, and the bear stopped. He lifted a finger with an upward movement and the bear stood on his hind legs.

"He's huge," hollered Cody.

Then Elen made a circular motion with his finger and the bear spun around and around, going faster and faster. Soon he was going so fast that all the children could see was a big black ball of blurry fuzz.

"I'm scared, Elen," said Lela with a shaky voice.

When Elen felt he had spun the bear enough, he stopped him. The bear turned and wobbled off in the opposite direction hitting a tree occasionally.

Elen howled with laughter. "That old bear looks like he's just eaten a keg full of rotten apples. How's that for a drunken old fool?" asked Elen.

Cody looked at Elen with a puzzled glance. "What happens when the apples are rotted, Elen?"

"They ferment and turn into a form of wine. If you eat them or make juice it's like liquor. It will get you drunk," said Elen.

"I'm sure glad you could stop him, Elen," said Cody.

"Me too," said Lela. "I was scared."

"Yeah, it would have been a little tough for Pere to get through the thick trees overhead," said Elen.

The children glanced up at the thick, tangled mass of limbs overhead.

"I won't ever be scared again, Elen," said Lela.

"Me either," said Cody.

"Well, don't ever say never," said Elen. Always prepare for the worst but hope for the best."

They headed back to Elen's hut. When they arrived, the children jumped off and rushed to Tivvy. They wanted to tell their parents about seeing the bear. "Bye, Elen, the children called out."

When they arrived home, they burst through the door. "Mom, Dad, you should have seen the huge bear we saw in the forest," said Cody.

"Yeah, Mommy, Elen made him go in circles until he was drunk," said Lela

"Drunk?" asked Robin.

"He wasn't drunk, Mom, just dizzy from the long spin around Elen gave him," said Cody.

Bob and Robin laughed. "You children are very fortunate to have Elen as a friend. You can enjoy seeing and going different places."

On Saturday Bob and the children took lumber into the forest for the tree house.

Elen saw Bob drive in and went out to greet them. "Super Bob, super, this wood looks great. We should have quite a mansion once we're finished." Elen turned to the children. "Now, tell me little ones, where is this mansion going to be built?" asked Elen.

"The children looked around, "Over there," piped Lela as she pointed to a large oak tree diagonally across from Elen's hut. "I'd like it there too and make it as high as you can, Elen," said Cody.

"I'm in agreement, and the oak is a much better decision than a pine," said Bob, especially since it'll be right across from you Elen."

As Elen lay on his blanket after nightfall overtook the forest, he listened to frogs croaking, crickets chirping and the lone call of an owl. He looked further into the forest and saw lights flashing off and on. His curiosity got the best of him so he got up and stepped out of the hut. He watched for a while then ran to catch one. When he caught it, he cupped it in his hands and peeked in. "I'll be a hornswoggled horned toad, they're some kind of beetle. Look at them, Pere, they look like sparkles of light scattered out like stars in the night don't they? It's beautiful and magical."

"They sure do," said Pere.

"That's really something. I've never seen anything like it. Super, I like it, super," said Elen.

A month later Elen finished the tree house then made a rope ladder for the children to climb. He and Pere flew to the Smith home and knocked on the door.

Cody answered the door. "Lela, Elen's here!" hollered Cody. "Come on in Elen."

Lela screamed joyfully, climbed on the banister and slid down until she reached the bottom of the stairs. "Hi, Elen," she shouted.

"Hi, Princess, did you ever find that dead egg?" asked Elen smiling.

Lela laughed and ran to Elen. "You knew, Elen. You knew what my teacher meant, why didn't you tell me?" asked Lela.

"Well, it's like this Princess, I thought it would give me more time to build the tree house so I kept my mouth shut."

Lela slapped at him teasingly.

Elen winked at the children. "Well, your tree house is ready, there's just one problem."

"Oh, no," said Lela.

"What is it?" asked Cody.

"You'll have to come with me to find out."

The children stood and looked at him questionably wondering what the problem was.

"Well, are you just going to stand there? Your taxi waits," said Elen.

"I'm ready, let's go," yelled Cody.

When they arrived in the forest, the children gasped. "Elen, It's beautiful; it's a castle in a tree, I love it," shouted Lela.

"What's wrong with it, Elen," asked Cody.

"I was joshing; just giving you a bad time. Do you like it?"

"Yes," the children chimed together.

"What are you waiting for? Your castle is calling," said Elen.

The children ran to the castle and began climbing the rope ladder, grabbed a handle and stepped inside. "I love it, Elen, it's beautiful. I could live here forever," cried Lela. "I do too," said Cody looking out a window. "The forest looks so different from up here."

"I'm so happy you like it. The steps were made of rope so you can pull them up at night to keep strangers out."

"Thank you, Elen," said Lela. "I love it and I love you."

"I love you too, Elen. Thank you," said Cody.

The sun rose in the morning with a delightful golden glow of yellow touched with a soft pink. Elen grabbed some cracked acorns. He'd been working on this plan since he had moved into the forest. He placed the acorns across a fallen log and fetched watercress out of the brook then sat down and waited while he munched on the spicy plant. Within an hour the squirrels spotted the acorns and began eating.

Each day Elen brought acorns, placing them on the same log and sat under the same tree talking to them. They began getting used to seeing Elen, As soon as he sat down they started climbing over him looking for nuts. He became their pied piper. They followed him through the forest almost every day.

One morning when Elen exited his hut, a squirrel sat waiting for him. "Well, have you come to be my friend?" Elen went back into the hut and fetched nuts for him. This continued for several days. Then one night, Elen was awakened when something crawled on him. He sat up and saw the squirrel. "Okay, my little friend, if you're going to be hanging around me we have to give you a name." While Elen thought about a name, he fed him nuts.

The next morning the squirrel was in the hut with him again. Elen began feeding him nuts. "I thought of a name for you, little friend. How do you like Feanaro? It means "friend" in elf language. Do you like it?" Fenanaro looked up at Elen and chattered. Elen let out a peal of laughter. "All right, Feanaro it is," said Elen.

10

Revenge

Jake was furious when Elen walked out and he wasn't about to let him get by with it. He punched in his friend's phone number.

"Charlie? It's Jake. Hey, I have a job for you. Elen left and I think he's staying in the forest. I need you to check it out. Nobody, but nobody walks out on Jake Jennings."

After his call, Jake pulled the overhead ladder down and went upstairs to a large antique trunk and opened it. He took out several pieces of gold and went back downstairs then lifted the ladder back in place.

The next day, at Jake's request, Charlie was in the forest looking for Elen and a possible campsite. He hid behind thickets at the brook, knowing Elen would need water if he was, in fact, living in the forest.

When Elen showed up, Charlie watched him while he fetched a pail of water. When he left the brook, Charlie followed, cautiously, slipping behind trees until Elen reached his campsite. What he saw at the campsite blew his mind. Shocked, he took off to Jake's shack.

Charlie entered the shack breathing heavily. "You won't believe what I just saw, Jake."

"What was it?"

"Elen on a flying reindeer and not only does it fly, but it is blue!" said Jake.

"You're joshing me, Charlie," said Jake.

"Nope, I'm not. Saw it with my own eyes. Elen jumped on the reindeer and they took off into the air," said Charlie still huffing. "What are your plans?"

"Oh, my word, that changes the whole picture. What a piece of luck." Jake rubbed his hands together. "Come to Papa, baby. That reindeer is worth big bucks." Jake stood silent for a moment with his hand cupped on his chin while thinking.

"Hmm, I have a friend with a helicopter. I'll see if he'll let me borrow it. We'll take Elen up about 500 feet over the canyon and drop him off and he can kiss his little fanny goodbye.

Since he's from the North Pole, no one is going to miss him. I'll find out when the helicopter is available," said Jake.

"Will it be done after dark?" asked Charlie.

"Of course, darkness is our friend. I'll get a pair of night goggles so you'll be able to find your way through the forest. I'll have a blanket and bungee cords to wrap him in. You'll have to make sure the reindeer is away from his campsite before you snatch him."

"Okay, it sounds like you have it planned. Let me know when you're ready Charlie, Jake said as he turned to leave."

"Sure, I'll keep in touch."

Charlie paused for a moment then turned around to face Jake. "Uh, oh, by the way, Jake, on second thought, I'll only help if I get one-half of the sale price," said Charlie with his eyes darting back and forth.

Jake's eyebrows arched. "What? You want a whole half of the sale?" That's kind of steep isn't it, Charlie?"

"Well, it's work to spy day in and day out and take my life into my own hands. Take it or leave it, Jake."

"Okay, okay, I'll take it." Jake reached into his pocket and pulled out the gold coins and handed them to Charlie. "Here's your pay for the last job, thanks."

The more Jake thought about the blue reindeer and the amount of money Charlie asked for, he couldn't handle the pressure. *There must be another way. Besides, he wasn't sure Charlie was telling the truth. He had to see the reindeer for himself. If he could entice Elen to live with him again, he'd have access to the reindeer.*

Jake headed into the forest. He found Elen at the pond. "Elen, hey man, I came to apologize for being such a jerk. I'd like for you to come back. The forest is no place to live." said Jake.

"Not in a million years. Leopards don't change their spots. What is it you really want, Jake?" asked Elen.

"Nothing at all, I just feel bad about the way things worked out. What do you say?" asked Jake.

"Yeah right; tell me another one," said Elen.

"Well, think about it. I'll see you around," and Jake turned to leave.

Elen started to get up when Jake whirled around and shoved him into the pond. Jake held him under water while Elen fought to come up. When he was able to come up momentarily, Elen gasped for air and yelled. "PERE, PERE, HELP!"

Jake pushed him under again, holding him down. Pere flew into Jake giving him a good swift butt with his antlers that sent him sailing to the middle of the pond. Jake swam to the other side and got out. He looked back to see the blue reindeer.

Elen hung on to Pere as they proceeded to get out of the pond. "I guess you're right, Elen, there is someone that doesn't like you. I would definitely say he isn't a friend. Are you okay?" asked Pere.

"Yeah, just a little shaken. Thanks, Pere."

"No problem, friend."

11

A Brush with Evil

The children dashed into the forest riding Tivvy on Saturday morning to visit Elen and Pere, but there was no sign of them. "I wonder where they are," said Cody.

"Let's go to the tree house and wait for them, Cody," said Lela. They climbed the rope ladder into the tree house and Cody pulled up the rope. They colored and read books for hours but Elen and Pere never showed up.

"Maybe they're at Jake's house," said Lela.

"Yeah, they probably are. Let's ride over to see if we can find his place," said Cody. "I'd like to see where Elen lived anyway." Cody had an idea where it was so they began their journey. They arrived about an hour later but there was no sign of anyone around.

"What a dump!" cried Lela.

"Yeah, not much to look at, for sure," said Cody. "Let's go in and take a look around."

"I-I don't know. We really shouldn't, Cody"

"Awe, come on, just for a moment."

"Okay, but just for a minute."

They slid off Tivvy and stepped onto the creaky porch. Cody turned the knob and opened the door. The children glanced around.

"Not much of a place to stay but he had a roof over his head," said Cody. He spotted a pull-down ladder on the ceiling. "Hey, let's see what's upstairs."

"No, Cody, we have to go. I'm scared."

Cody ignored his sister and jumped up and pulled the ladder down. "Come on, sis, we'll only be a minute."

"That's what you said a while ago. Let's go, Cody!" yelled Lela.

"Not before I see what's up there. Come on, Lela, be a sport." Cody climbed the stairs and Lela reluctantly followed.

"What a bunch of junk!" said Cody. He spotted an old machine in the corner and wandered over to it.

Lela saw a trunk and lifted the lid. "Oh, my gosh, Cody, look! It's a treasure chest full of silver and gold."

"Lela, come here, quick," shouted Cody. Lela sauntered over to the machine. "What is it?" she asked.

"It's an old printing press of some sort." Cody glanced over and spotted green paper. "I'll be doggone."

"What? What is it?"

Cody picked up some green paper. "It's money."

"Money?" asked Lela.

"It's money all right, but it's fake money. Real money isn't printed in someone's house. Only the government can print it. We'd better get outta here, NOW" said Cody, then he heard a car. "Oh, no, it's too late." He ran to the window and saw a car drive in. "We're in deep doo-doo, come on Lela, run and run fast. Whatever you do, don't stop running."

Lela followed Cody down the stairs. Cody slammed the ladder up against the ceiling and was out the door. Lela was caught by the arm by Jake before she got out.

"Let me go, let me go," shouted Lela.

"What are you two scoundrels doing in my house?" yelled Jake. Lela fought to get loose but Jake had a firm grip.

Outside, Cody heard Lela's screams. He ran back up the stairs and into the house.

"Let her go you coward" yelled Cody. He picked up a broom and began hitting Jake.

Jake was trying to keep his hold on Lela but he was also fighting the broom. Lela finally sank her teeth into Jake's arm. He yelled and let go. Lela and Cody fled out of the house. Cody jumped onto Tivvy and pulled Lela up behind him and took off like a shot. "You all right, little sis?" yelled Cody.

"I-I'm scared to death, Cody, and I peed my pants!" she yelled back.

"We'll go straight home," he hollered.

When they got home, Lela went upstairs to shower and change clothes. She was still shaking from the nightmare they had just lived when she went downstairs.

"Have a seat, little sis; I'll make you some hot chocolate. Maybe it'll calm you down. That was some experience wasn't it?" asked Cody.

Lela flipped out. "Yeah, and it's your fault, Cody. We could have been hurt or killed," she screamed. "I told you I didn't want to go in, and look what happened. I'll never forget it, and I'll never forgive you. I'm madder than a wet hen in a foxes den."

"Calm down, Lela. We got out, and we're all right. That's all that matters."

"Yeah, right, but if Daddy ever finds out, we'll both be skinned alive."

That night Elen laid thinking while watching the silvery clouds drifting overhead. *He reasoned the bratty bird must have some awareness of the value of silver to bring it to him. He didn't know, but he did know it was a sign of goodness.*

"I'll think of a name for the bird. Who knows, he might become a friend too," said Elen. He looked at Pearl. "What do you think, little girl?"

"I think he might not want to be your friend after you packed such a wallop on his little rump. He probably thinks you're a monster. If I'd been in his position, and it was my rump, I wouldn't come within a mile of you."

Elen grinned and reached over and patted Pearl on the head. "Time will tell, girl, but I'll think of a name just in case."

Elen awoke to beautiful weather the next morning. It was sunny and warm with rich scents of pine and wild honeysuckle. He fed Feanaro and Pearl and left the hut. Pearl and Feanaro followed. He saw Pere grazing and hollered. "Hey, Pere, let's take a walk to the water."

"Okay, Elen, something on your mind?"

"Yes. Maybe a little fresh air will jog my brain. I'm trying to think of a name for that feisty little bird."

"Oh, you're going to name him? Hope it's a nicer name than he's been called," said Pere.

"Come on, Pere, give me a break." They walked along the trampled trail they had made from frequent visits to the brook. Once there, Elen sat on his usual stump. While Pere was sipping water, Elen was deep in thought then suddenly he said, "Aha, he's a she so I'm going to name her Eurane."

Pere looked up at Elen. *By the shades of heaven, how did Elen know the bird was a female?*

About that time, Elen spotted the bird and latched on to his hat. "Not this time, Eurane," he said. She landed on a tree across the brook, ruffled her feathers and flew away.

12

A Thief in the Night

The night was cool; the air was crisp. A half-moon offered enough light for a stealth figure to slip through the forest. He spotted his target and approached him quietly. He hoped to throw a rope around Pere's neck but the attempt failed when it caught just one antler.

Frightened, Pere jumped and rose up immediately. He flew to Elen's hut with the man dangling from his antlers. "Elen, Elen, wake up. We have a thief in the night." Elen slept on.

"ELENNNN, WAKE UP!" yelled Pere.

Elen stirred and opened his eyes. He went to the opening of the hut and looked at Pere. He rubbed his eyes not believing what he saw. "Wh- What's that you have, Pere?"

"A would be thief, and one that's not good with a lasso. What shall I do with him?" asked Pere.

"Bring him on down. I have a few questions." Elen found himself face to face with an old man. His eyes were dark and wisps of white hair shown from beneath his cap. "Just what did you think you were gonna do old man?" asked Elen.

The old man narrowed his eyes. "I ain't talkin."

"Who are you tryin' to protect, old man?" asked Elen.

"I ain't talkin," he said again.

"Hmm, you want me to find out the hard way?" asked Elen.

"Whatdoya mean, the hard way?"

"Can you dance old man?" asked Elen.

"No, what kind of games you tryin' to play?" the old man inquired.

"No games, but I can teach you to dance." Elen zapped bolts of electricity at his feet.

The old man started hopping, jumping and turning in circles to keep from getting hit. Elen gave him a final zap on his rump.

"Ouch," screamed the old man. "If you didn't have magic, you wouldn't be such a whiz-bang kid, would you?"

"Call me what you like. Why were you trying to steal Pere?"

"Well, now, I reckon you'll have to figure that out all by yourself hocus-pocus man."

"Wait a minute? I've seen you before." Elen thought for a moment. "Oh, yes, Pere and I were flying, and you were watching from the road. Heed my warning old man, you dare not return, or I'll make you look like a cooked turkey," Elen said in a tone that left no happy medium.

The old man felt his legs starting to wobble. He had a knot in the pit of his stomach, but he managed to start running before this fool turned him into something that resembled road kill. *There wasn't enough money in the world to make it worth getting himself killed, he thought.*

Elen looked at Pere and they burst out laughing. "We sure bamboozled that old man. I guess we'd better call it a night, my friend."

"A great Idea, I'll see you in the morning," said Pere.

Elen smiled and took a deep breath running his fingers through his hair before he entered the hut. He lay down but sleep wouldn't come. The thought of someone trying to steal Pere put too much stress on him. He tossed and turned the rest of the night.

After Elen arose in the morning, he stepped out into the brilliant sunlight.

"Good morning, Pere. I was awake the rest of the night after our little episode."

"You were, why?"

"I was thinking about you, listening to frogs, the crickets, the hoot of an owl the call of a coyote and all the sounds of mother nature. It's truly a blessing, something I'd never hear at the North Pole. I'd like to say I want to stay, but I can't."

"I love it too, I'll never go back home. Don't you think you'll get used to it and accept living here?" asked Pere.

"I don't know, Pere. I think I could, maybe, but I have a strange feeling inside that I can't seem to shake."

"Like what, Elen?"

"I can't explain it. A feeling of doom and gloom, I guess. It's like a race against time, and I don't know what it means. It's one of the reasons I feel compelled to go home."

"Give it some time, maybe it will work itself out," said Pere.

13

The Arsonist

The next day as Elen hunted, he had a thought. "Hey, Pere, you know we're just a few miles away from the beach and we've never seen it. We can fly over at early dawn in a forsaken spot and take some time off. I've been so stressed lately. What do you think?"

Pere snickered. "It sounds cool and like lots of fun. Let's do it."

Elen arose in the early morning. He stepped outside and took a deep breath and stretched his arms. There was a faint whiff of burning leaves in the air; a sure sign of autumn around the corner. Pere pranced over.

"You still want to go to the beach today?" asked Pere.

"Yep, we'll find a secluded area. Let's be off as soon as I have a bite to eat."

Elen fed Feanaro, Pearl and himself and then jumped onto Pere and called to Pearl.

"Come on, girl, jump. He slapped at his leg. She hesitated. He slapped again. "Come on girl, let's go." Pearl jumped, and Elen caught her in his arms. Pere flew until no one was in sight. *Not many people around, thought Elen. Since it was cool, it probably kept* them off *the beach.* Pere landed and Elen hopped off.

Later that morning Cody and Lela rode into the forest to visit Elen and Pere but there was no sign of them. "They're gone." said Lela. "I wonder where they went this time."

"I don't know. Let's go to the tree house and read until they get back," said Cody. He tied Tivvy to a tree and they climbed the ladder into the tree house. Cody pulled the steps up behind them. They played with their activity books and read while waiting

When Pere arrived at the beach, Elen and Pearl jumped down. "Look at the sand, Pere, Its white as snow." He reached down and grabbed a handful and threw it into the air then looked out over the ocean. "Wow, this is beautiful, I've never seen anything like this."

Elen slipped out of his shoes and ran into the water. "Yahooo!" he screamed. Pere and Pearl ran in after him prancing and dancing in the water. Elen splashed Pere and Pere lifted a leg and brought it down splashing water on Elen.

"Do you smell the sea?" Elen asked Pere.

"I surely do, it has a refreshing smell, doesn't it?"

They laughed and played for hours then Elen sat down in the sand and watched the waves froth and splash onto the beach while Pere and Pearl chased one another. Suddenly Pearl stopped. Her ears perked up and she sniffed the air.

While Lela read, she heard a noise. She got up and looked out the window and backed away. "Cody," she whispered, "There's a man down there."

Cody arose and peeked out. "Sit down and keep quiet," mumbled Cody. "I've seen him before," whispered Cody.

"What's he looking for?" asked Lela.

"Shh!" said Cody. He watched as the man moved around poking into Elen's belongings. He untied Tivvy and slapped her on the rump sending her galloping home.

"What's he looking for?" Lela asked again.as she stood up and looked out. "I don't like him, he scares me. Why did he chase Tivvy away?"

"Shhh! Lela! Shut up and sit down. You're going to give us away and then we'll have a real problem." Lela backed up and sat down.

Cody watched the man empty a can of liquid onto the ground as he was backing out of the forest. Soon the forest was on fire.

"Oh, no Lela, we've get outta here quick. That man set the forest on fire," yelled Cody.

Lela jumped up and looked out the window. "Cody, what are we going to do?"

"We have to make a run for it," screamed Cody.

"The fire is too fast, we can't, Cody, we don't have Tivvy," yelled Lela.

Cody looked out the window again. The fire was barreling towards them at a high rate of speed. "You're right, little sis, it's too fast. We're stuck here. I hope Elen and Pere get here before it's too late." He sat down and bowed his head in prayer.

As Elen sat enjoying the waves and watching Pere and Pearl play, he saw Pearl stop and perk up her ears. "What's wrong, girl?" Elen called to Pearl.

"I-I'm not sure...It...It's the chil....FIRE," she yelled.

"Oh, no!" cried Elen. He ran to Pere and jumped on and Pearl jumped into his arms.

"Go, Pere, go! Hurry, the children may be in danger."

As they got closer to the forest, the smoke thickened and Elen became frantic. By the time they got within a short distance they could see the forest was filled with smoke and fire. "Faster, Pere, faster," Elen yelled. "Take me to the Smith's place, quick!"

In the air Elen spotted Tivvy near the garage with her reins dangling. Pere landed in the back yard and Elen ran to the house. He knocked and called. "Lela! Cody!" He banged on the door but still no answer. He grabbed a chair and broke a window and crawled through. When he got inside, he found Bob's number at the college tacked on the wall near the phone and called him. "Bob, the forest is on fire and the children aren't here. I'm going into the forest to find them," and hung up.

Elen ran to the garage and grabbed ropes and hopped back onto Pere. "Fly to the tree house, Pere, hurry!" screamed Elen.

"But...."

"We gotta see if they're there, Pere, hurry!"

Pere entered the forest headed for the tree house and Elen's hut.

Elen called. **"CODYYYYY, LELAAAAA!** Pere continued deeper into the forest. When they got to the hut, it was in ashes. Elen cupped his hands around his mouth and called again. **"CODYYYYYY, LELAAAAAA!"**

"Up here, Elen, in the tree house!" yelled Cody. "Hurry, Elen, we can't breathe."

"Lay face down on the floor with your head cradled in your arms. Is Lela all right?" Elen called back.

"I don't know, she's not talking," Cody yelled between coughs.

"I'll be right there, hang tough!" yelled Elen.

"Pere, fly me as close to the tree house as you can get." When Elen was able to grab onto the door casing he worked his way inside and saw Lela was lying on the floor passed out He tied the rope around Lela and under her arms then picked her up. "I'm ready, Pere, come get us. I need you as close to the branch as possible. Lela is unconscious so I'll have to hold her while I climb on." He held onto her while Pere flew up to the door. He was able to straddle Pere with her in front of him then he called to Cody. "Cody, do you think you're able to get onto Pere? I can help with one hand," yelled Elen.

"Y-Yeh, I think so...I'll try," said Cody.

"Okay, I'm here to help."

"Pere get closer to the door if you can." Pere inched closer to the door and Elen reached out for Cody's hand. Cody tried reaching for Elen.

"I can't Elen," cried Cody, "I'm scared."

"You can do it Cody; Pere is our only way out. Try again. Your little sister is depending on you. You can save her life. Come on, give me your hand," coaxed Elen. Cody reached out again for Elen's hand. Elen saw the chance to grab it and leaned over as far as he dared while hanging onto Lela and grabbed it. "Jump, Cody, jump, straddle Pere. I've got you." Cody jumped and straddled Pere and grasped Elen's frail body tightly. "Go Pere, go," shouted Elen.

As they were leaving the forest, Elen heard the wailing of fire trucks and airplanes overhead dropping fire retardant and water on the fire. When they arrived on the lawn of the Smith home, Bob, Robin and the responders rushed to Pere lifting Lela and Cody off. They lay them on the ground and the medics began helping them. Once Elen saw they were being cared for he ran for the forest of trees.

Pere saw Elen running for the trees and yelled. "Elen, stop, you'll get yourself killed."

As Elen entered the forest, he began calling Pearl. He ran further, the smoke was getting thicker and it was hard for him to breathe so he took his red handkerchief from his pocket and held it over his nose. It seemed hours before he felt Pearl at his side. He grabbed her by her tail and she led him to safety. The family heard Pearl yipping and they looked up to see her leading Elen out of the forest.

Pere trotted to Elen. "Thank goodness you're all right. I was worried sick about you. That was a foolish thing to do," he said.

Bob and Robin rushed to Elen with hugs and kisses and humble thanks for saving the children.

"Are the children all right?" asked Elen.

Robin was crying. "Yes, Elen, thanks to you. Thank you for saving our little ones."

Elen looked down at Pearl. "Fianaro," he cried out. He stooped down and hugged Pearl and pet Fianaro. "Thank you Pearl for saving our friend, you are truly a life saver."

An officer stepped over to Elen. "I want to thank you for your actions Elen. You saved the children's lives. It was a very brave thing to do."

"I would do it a thousand times over, officer. I love those children."

After the officer left Elen's side, Bob and Robin also left to be near the children. Elen sat on the ground and watched the medics care for Cody and Lela. He was worried and had tears welling in his eyes. He looked over at Bob and Robin and they could see he was distressed so they went back to him. Robin sat down beside him and put her arm around him. Bob sat on his other side. "Are they going to be all right?" asked Elen with tears running down his cheeks.

"Yes Elen, they will be, thanks to you and Pere. We may have lost both of our precious children if it weren't for you," said Bob. Robin began crying again and hugged Elen harder.

"I wonder what started the fire," questioned Elen. "I feel so bad that I wasn't here when it started. I may have been able to prevent it."

"Elen, it's not your fault," said Robin. "Don't blame yourself. When the children get better, perhaps they can shed some light on what happened. We're just thankful you made it home in time to save them."

As they sat there watching, other fire trucks and an ambulance arrived at the scene. The children and Robin were placed in the ambulance and taken to the hospital with siren's blaring.

Bob and Elen prepared to follow them in the car. Elen called to Pere. "Take Pearl and Feanaro into the barn and wait for us to return," he said. He watched as Pere led them toward the barn.

After the children were released from the hospital, the family returned home. They gathered in the family room and discussed the fire. Elen couldn't believe what the children were telling them. He sat quietly and listened while thinking at the same time. When the children finished telling what they saw, Elen was deep in thought for a moment looking at the floor then he raised his head and asked Bob a question. "Bob, this was the third time that fellow has been in the forest and each time he was up to no good. Why do you suppose he's coming back again and again?"

"I'm not sure Elen unless he wants you out of the way because of Pere."

"Why would anyone want Elen out of the way, Dad?" asked Cody. Elen hasn't hurt anyone."

"I'm not really sure son. but if he saw Elen on Pere in flight, then he might want him out of the way so he could take Pere."

Elen's eyes popped wide open when he heard Bob. "Oh, heaven forbid Bob I think you've hit the nail on the head. There was a man on a road below when I took my first ride on Pere. He was watching us with his mouth wide open. I truly believe you are right." Elen paused for a moment, "Well, I think I'll mosey on home and sleep under the stars tonight."

"No, no, Elen, sleep in the tree house," said Cody.

"Yeah and make sure you pull the steps up so that mean old man can't get you," said Lela.

Elen smiled. "I think I could do more damage to him than he could do to me, Princess, but I'll sleep in the tree house. Thanks for your offer Cody. I'm sure happy everything turned out alright and you two little ones are safe. I'll borrow your tools tomorrow Bob and start the cleanup. Goodnight, all."

"Oh, wait," called Robin. She ran to the bedroom and brought out a sleeping bag and pillow and returned and handed it to Elen. "You'll need these, Elen."

"Thank you Robin, I appreciate it. It will be much more comfortable." Elen said as he turned to leave.

"Goodnight, Elen," the family chimed together. "I'll stop by after work and give you a hand, Elen," said Bob.

"Okay Bob." He waved his hand over his head as he walked out the door.

As Elen walked through the forest, he shook his head as he looked around. The only thing left was the blackened trees and the treehouse. *How ugly, he thought, but what a miracle it was the treehouse was saved along with the children.*

The family showed up the next morning with rakes and shovels to help with the forest clean-up. They worked through the day. Elen paused for a moment and looked at the hard-working family; he was so proud of them. "It doesn't take long with all of us working," he said.

"You're right about that," said Bob. We make a good team."

Weeks passed and as Christmas came nearer, the family became closer. Elen and Pere would travel into the forest to feed Fianaro and Elen would do more clean-up and work on a new hut he was building for himself then he'd return to the Smith home.

When the sun neared the horizon the next day, Elen took his fishing pole to the pond. He needed a break, and fishing was a relaxation for him.

Pere jogged up to Elen after trying to find a place to graze. "What a difference greenery makes in the forest. It's black and ugly now with no place to graze."

'You'll just have to travel further into the forest, Pere. Yeah, there sure is a difference alright. Hey, Pere, I have a confession to make."

"You, a confession? I can't believe you'd do anything wrong to have to confess my friend."

"It's not that kind of a confession but I'm not without fault. Something happened yesterday. Something inside me; you might call it a realization. After I saw the children in danger and they could possibly die, I became aware of how much the family means to me."

"Yeah?" said Pere.

"I know Santa and Mrs. Claus love me; they raised me from a newborn, but I never thought anyone else could love me, nor I love them. I have found that I love the children; they feel like a brother and sister;

something I've always longed for and I look at Bob and Robin as my parents. Am I making any sense?"

"Of course you are and you deserve their love but don't count me out."

Elen chuckled and shook his head. "Never in a million years my friend would I ever doubt neither your love for me nor my love for you. You are true blue and exceptional."

"There you go again mentioning my color."

Elen chuckled. "I love your color, it's beautiful. I think you are very special and I wouldn't change a thing about you."

After the children were settled in bed that night, Bob was reading the paper and Robin was knitting a sweater. Bob laid his paper face down on his lap. "Robin, I'm worried about Elen. It seems so many things are happening that is aimed at him."

Robin looked at Bob. "I think so too, Bob. Do you think it's because of Pere and his ability to fly?"

"That and the fact he's blue. He could fetch a pretty penny for some greedy person if they sold him to a circus."

"Oh, my goodness Bob, Elen would be overcome with grief if something like that happened. Is there anything we can do?"

"I'm not sure what the answer is. We'll have to keep a watchful eye out. Perhaps one day soon we'll have an answer."

"I sure hope so Bob. It not only involves us, but also the children."

14

Snowy Mountain

The family had been working day after day in the forest cleaning up the debris and planting new trees that Bob had bought. Elen had built himself a new hut and Pere had to travel a little further to graze but they had made the same place in the forest their home.

In their spare time Lela had been practicing trick riding for a rodeo and Bob was teaching Cody how to play the guitar.

After the devastating fire and the children's narrow escape, Elen wanted to take the children on a special trip so he and Pere flew to the Smith home.

Elen knocked on the door and Robin answered. "Hi Elen, come on in and have a seat. I'll fetch a cup of coffee for you." Elen smiled and tipped his hat. "Thanks, Robin."

As soon as the children heard Elen's voice, they scrambled down the stairs to greet him. "Hi Elen," said Cody. "What's your plan for the day? Are we planting more trees?" he asked.

Elen smiled and winked. "No, I think it's time for a break. I came over to see if we could take you and Lela on a trip."

"You did, Elen, you really did? You're going to take us on a trip? Where to?" asked Lela excitedly.

"Well, of course, we have to get Mom and Dad's permission before we go anywhere," said Elen realizing he was referring to Bob and Robin as Mom and Dad.

"Can we Mommy; can we go on a trip with Elen?" Lela asked bubbling over with excitement.

"Yeah, I'd like to go somewhere too, shouted Cody. We've been working our booties off," he said laughing.

At that time, Bob entered the room. "What's all the excitement about?" he asked.

"Elen wants to take us on a trip, Daddy. Can we go, please?" asked Lela.

Bob smiled and greeted Elen with a nod. "Well, where will you be going?" asked Bob.

Cody shrugged his shoulders and they looked at Elen.

"I think the children should decide. Where would you like to go or what would you like to see?" asked Elen. "Is there anything you've never seen that you'd love to see?"

The children looked at each other; then Cody shouted, "The snow, Elen, the snow."

"Yes, yes, yes," Lela shouted in agreement jumping up and down. "We've never seen the snow."

"Never, really, geez, we had so much snow at the North Pole I felt like I was buried in it. Okay, the snow it is, if it's all right with Mom and Dad." said Elen. *There I go again, calling them Mom and Dad. I hope they don't mind, thought Elen.*

Lela jumped up and down with excitement then started twirling around. "Elen, look at me, look at me."

Elen smiled impishly and made a circular motion with a finger and she started spinning her faster until her dress clung to her small body. "Yep, I see you all right; you look like an out-of-control spinning top." He stopped her and she staggered around. Everyone laughed.

"Now I understand why you thought the bear was drunk, Lela," said Bob laughing.

"You tricked me, Elen, you made me go faster," squealed Lela.

"Yep, I'm guilty as charged. I love you Princess; come and give me a hug." Lela ran to him and hugged him tightly around his neck. "Well, I guess we'd better hit the road; I have things to do at the home place. We'll see you little ones on Saturday."

Saturday morning Elen and Pere were at the house early. The children ran out the door and were excited when they arrived. "Hi there, little ones" said Elen greeting them.

"We're ready to go," shouted Lela.

"Yep, I see that. You look like little Eskimos," Elen said smiling.

Cody helped Elen pack food and water into the saddlebag along with a flashlight and matches.

"Here's a warm jacket for you Elen," said Robin handing it to him. "I picked it up the other day, I hope it fits," she said.

"Thank you, Robin," he said as he put on the coat. "You're very thoughtful. We'll take good care of the children." Elen turned and helped the children onto Pere then handed Pearl to Cody. He jumped onto Pere's rump and soon they were high above the forest.

The children were in awe as they traveled over cities, hills and dales seeing sights they had never seen before. Soon they spotted snow over the Smokey Mountains in Tennessee. "Cody, look there's snow. It's so pretty and white," Lela hollered.

"Wow, it's beautiful," cried Cody.

"Yep, it surely is a beautiful blanket of crystal-white snow," said Elen. "Pere look for a nice landing place," said Elen.

Pere slowly lowered his altitude. The children squirm on his back with excitement. When Pere landed, the children jumped off and began throwing snowballs.

"Let's build a snowman," yelled Cody. They rolled a large ball of snow. When they thought it was big enough, they started another ball for the head. When they finished, Cody tried placing it atop the big one but he wasn't tall enough to accomplish it. "I guess we made him too big," he cried.

Ellen walked over and picked up the snowball and placed it on the larger one. The children searched for limbs for his arms and rocks for his eyes then stood back and admired their handy work.

"Hey, let's make snow angels, Lela," said Cody. He lay down in the snow and moved his arms and legs then Lela lay down and did the same. They laughed and screamed to the top of their lungs. Suddenly Lela sat up and looked around. "What's that noise, Elen?" she asked.

Elen glanced up at the top of the mountain and became frantic. "Run! Go to Pere, quick!"

Elen ran to Pere and quickly lifted the children onto his back then he jumped on his rump. "Go, Pere, go!" Elen yelled.

Pere shot up out of the snow. Lela and Cody looked back and saw snow beginning to slide down the side of the mountain.

"Whew, that was a close call," said Elen. "Too close for comfort."

"Why was the snow sliding down the mountain, Elen?" asked Cody.

"It was an avalanche. You can be buried alive in one of those."

Lela looked back again and this time it looked like a huge cloud floating down the mountain.

Pere flew to another area. When they landed, Elen pulled a blanket out of the saddlebag and spread it on top of the ground and they sat down to have lunch.

After lunch, they played snow tag. Elen started it off by throwing a snowball at Lela. "You're it, Lela." Lela screamed and picked up snow and made a ball and threw it at Cody. "You're it, Cody," she hollered and the game went on until suddenly, the ground caved in. Elen heard the screams of the children as they fell.

It seemed forever before they landed. Elen looked up toward the light in the gap overhead. He frantically glanced around and spotted Pere and ran to him. He opened the saddlebag in search of the flashlight. He fumbled around until he felt it. He turned it on and flashed it around looking for the children. "This was not our day," he grumbled fearfully.

"Cody! Lela!" he called out. There was no answer so he called again. "CODY, LELA," he called louder.

"I-I'm over here, Elen," yelled Cody.

Elen flashed the light over and saw Cody buried in mud waist high. He ran to him.

"Have you seen or heard Lela?" Elen asked frantically.

"No, I haven't, Elen."

"Pere, help dig Cody out while I search for Lela."

"We'll get him out, go find Lela, hurry!"

Elen flashed his light around. "Lela," he called but there was no answer. "Lelaaaaaa!" He called again and still no answer. "LELA, LELAAAAA," he called louder. "Please answer, Princess, can you hear me?" He stood silently and listened but there was no answer. He became panicked. Frantically, he began digging where the light hit the ground from above. He dug like a dog would dig for a bone while tears streamed down his face then suddenly, he stopped and listened. *Was that Lela he had heard?* He listened again shining the light around.

"Up here, Elen, I'm up here. I'm scared, please help me," she cried.

Elen shined the light up and saw her on a ledge sobbing. "Pere," he called out. "Are you free? Lela needs you to help her down from a ledge."

"Yeah, be there in a moment, just about through digging Cody out."

When Pere finished he went to Elen and he shined the light on Lela. Pere flew up and Lela grabbed onto his antlers and straddled him and he brought her down. Once the children were safe, Elen brought them close and hugged them but wouldn't speak for fear his voice would break.

"That was scary, Elen," said Cody.

Elen swallowed. "Yes, it was very scary and I'm so thankful we're all safe. Well, little ones, you did get to see the snow, but we got to see a lot more than we bargained for didn't we? I hope it wasn't so frightening that you'll never want to take another trip." Elen looked around while shining the light here and there. "I guess we'd better find out where we are, and how we're going to get out."

"Is this a cave, Elen?" asked Cody.

"It's dark in here, I'm scared, Elen," cried Lela. "Are there bears in here?"

"We're fine Princess. I doubt there are any bears but we can handle them if there is. Hang tough. I think it's an underground cave or perhaps a tunnel. Stay very close to me." Elen paused once in a while to get his bearings as to where they were and shined the light upward. "Oh, look," he shouted, "we're in a cave. See the stalactites?"

"Wow, they're beautiful," said Cody.

"Hey, Pere, does your guidance system work here?" asked Elen.

"So far, so good," answered Pere. "We're heading west."

"Great, it will get us out of here."

Cody turned to look at Pere and his eyes were glowing. "Pere, why are your eyes glowing?' he asked.

Pere chuckled. "All animals have better eyesight at night than they do during the day. We absorb more ultra-violet light than humans do. That's how they catch their prey at night."

Elen came to a stop and listened. "Shhhh, I think I hear water. Let's go this way. Cody, hold your sister's hand."

"I am, Elen."

As they walked, the sound of water became louder. Elen moved at a snail's pace not knowing what lies ahead He shined the light ahead and saw the water. "Look! It's an underground waterfall. It's beautiful. Come up near me little ones but watch your step." They watched in awe as the water, with touches of color, cascaded down the side of the mountain and disappeared into a crevice. Elen shined the light at the ceiling. "See the crescent shape up there?" A filter of light showed through at the top of the falls. "That's where the touches of color come from with the help of the sun. It's awesome. This is so amazing. I wonder how long this cave has been here."

"Years and years," said Pere.

Cody looked at Pere, "How do you know that, Pere," he asked.

"From the sizes of the stalactites and since they only grow with each drop of water it takes many, many years for them to be this big."

"He's right," said Elen.

"How many years do you think it took to make one that long?" asked Cody as he pointed to one.

"Well, I'd say it probably grows close to one-eighth of an inch per year and since the longest one is about eighteen inches, I figure it took about one-hundred and forty-four years," said Elen.

"Wow, that's awesome," said Cody.

"Will we find a pot of gold, Elen?" questioned Lela.

Pere snickered.

"Probably not a chance, Princess, you don't see a rainbow underground," said Elen.

"What makes the stalactites grow, Elen," asked Cody.

"A constant supply of water rich in calcium carbonate and carbon dioxide is what does it; minerals that come from the ground."

"What time is it Cody?" Elen shined the flashlight at Cody's watch.

"It's almost three o'clock."

"We'd better find a way out and start back. I don't want your mom and dad to worry. Pere, since you're the one with the GPS, can you come up and lead us out?" asked Elen.

"Sure, can do, will do, and have done," Pere said as he stepped up to the front to lead.

Once they found their way out of the cave, Pere flew into the Smith's back yard to unpack the saddlebag and greet the parents.

When they entered the house, Elen approached Bob and Robin. "We had a great time, had some wild moments but we saw and learned a lot today. Thanks for letting the children go. They can tell you all about it. We'll see everyone soon," said Elen and he and Pere left for the forest.

When they arrived at the hut, Elen dismounted. "What a wonderful but wild day," said Elen.

"Goodness yes, Elen, I'm looking forward to going back to explore the cave again."

"Yep, it was a mystery all right. I'd like to know more about it too. You did save the location on your GPS, didn't you, Pere?"

"By guess and by golly, I surely did."

15

Black Gold

It had been a while since Cody and Lela had their disagreement after going to Jake's shack. Lela had overcome her anger with her brother and they were back on good terms.

Cody had exploring fever again so he went to Lela's room and knocked.

Lela opened the door.

"Lela, let's go into the forest tomorrow to do some exploring. We can leave right after Dad and Mom do."

"What are we going to look for, another shack?" Lela asked with her green eyes sparkling. They laughed.

"I don't know," said Cody, "but we have three hundred acres to explore. There's no telling what we'll find. We'll ride Tivvy so we can travel faster."

"Daddy would get real upset if he found out. We're not supposed to go into the forest and you know it, Cody. The last time I listened to you we got into trouble. If we went in again and he found out, we wouldn't see daylight for months or Elen and Pere either. I don't want to go."

"I know, little sis, but the forest is our oyster. It's beautiful, wild and mysterious and you're the only one I have to go with. I can't handle being cooped up all the time. Come on, it'll be exciting, I promise. No telling what we could find while we're exploring."

Lela giggled. "Right big brother and we might get lost and not find our way back before Mommy and Daddy get home too."

"I'll see if Dad's compass is in the garage. We'll take it with us so we can get back."

"I-I don't know. I'm not sure it's a good idea. My heart tells me to stay but my head tells me to go. I-I really don't think we should, Cody."

"Awe, come on little sis. We'll have a good time and see a lot of different trees and other things. Please? I'll bring a rope, the compass, and an ax. We'll take the spray again too in case we run across a wild animal. We can pack a lunch and a table cloth and have a good time. We'll be back in time for Mom and Dad to be home, I promise."

Lela was hesitant. "Well, okay, I guess, but you'd better keep your promise."

"I will. Let's get busy with the sandwiches." They packed sandwiches and bottled water, a sheet to use as a tablecloth and other things they might need. Cody also packed a come-a-long in the saddle bag and binoculars. He wanted to be prepared for anything. Lela changed to her dungarees and a long sleeved shirt for protection.

Cody saddled up Tivvy and placed a rope around the horn of the saddle. He loaded the saddlebag onto the horse and climbed on then pulled Lela up in back of him. As they traveled, Cody occasionally checked the direction they were going on the compass. After charting their course and moving ahead an hour later, Lela heard a high-pitched cry coming from some animal in pain or some kind of trouble.

"Cody, what's that?" They heard it again.

"It's coming from over there," said Cody pointing to the west. He turned the horse in the direction of the sound. They kept on the trampled path following the sound. They finally came upon a doe trapped in a muddy swamp that had an awful smell. Lela slid off the horse and ran to the swamp.

"Oh, poor thing," she cried. She started to step into the pond when Cody hollered.

"Lela! Don't go in there! We don't know why she's trapped. We don't want to wind up in the same situation." Cody dismounted and went to stand by Lela to observe the situation. He reached down into the swamp. "That's pretty heavy, stinky stuff. It almost feels like sand. It could be quicksand and we don't want to find out the hard way. It's a good thing we brought a rope and the come-a-long. We're going to need it."

"What's a come-along, Cody?"

"It's a wheel with a set of teeth. It has a handle that you push and pull and it will bring her out of the swamp. I have to lasso her first then attach the lasso to the come-a-long."

Cody grabbed the come-a-long out of the saddlebag and placed it around a strong tree near the swamp. He created a lasso with the rope. When he was ready, he circled the lasso overhead and roped the deer. He tied the end of the rope to the come-a-long and proceeded to ratchet her in to land.

Lela watched her brother with pride. She'd never seen him so strong and confident. She swept back her long flowing blond hair as the soft wind blew it across her face. "I'm so happy you were able to help her, Cody. She might have died if we hadn't found her."

"If it's quicksand, nothing could have saved her. Now I understand why Dad keeps telling us it's dangerous in the forest. We have to keep a watchful eye as we travel," said Cody.

After they got the deer onto land, Cody talked to her and petted her to calm her down. He took the lasso from around her neck. Once freed, the doe trotted off to another part of the forest. Cody gathered the rope and placed it around the horn on the saddle then put the come-a-long back in the saddlebag. They mounted Tivvy and moved on.

When the sun was directly overhead, they stopped in a shady glen to eat and rest a bit. The meadow was alive with flowers in all shapes and colors. The humming of the insects filled the air as did the sweet scent of the blossoms. Bluebirds circled waiting for tidbits of bread to drop so they could swoop down and eat them.

"This is beautiful, Cody. I wonder why we don't see bluebirds at home."

"They probably feel much safer here in the forest. I love to explore new places; places where no one has been before," said Cody.

Lela smiled. "Do you think you'll be an explorer when you grow up?"

"I don't know, but it sounds like fun. We'd better hit the trail. I think we'll travel another hour or so then we'll start home."

They picked up their mess and started out again. They passed through a meadow where the waving grass stood nearly as high as Lela's shoulders. The land rolled on, beautiful and wild; most of it covered with a forest of trees. Lela felt a pang of love for her father's land and its unspoiled beauty. She now understood why her brother was excited about exploring it.

Trails wound around squishy paths, past huge vine-draped trees where little creatures skittered up and down the bark on trees. Cody spotted what he thought was a mud hole about the width of two yards wide and he noticed something strange happening. He stopped and they slid off Tivvy. He tied her to a tree and they sauntered over to the bubbling circle. Cody squatted down to examine it. He stuck his finger into the thick liquid and pulled it out. It was dark and greasy. He looked at his sister. "Lela, I think we've just discovered oil."

"Oh, geez, Cody, what are we going to do? We can't tell Daddy because we'll get into deep trouble."

Cody looked at his little sister. "We'll have to tell Elen and have him check it out." He looked at the compass and memorized their location. "We'd better start back now so we'll get home before Mom and Dad arrive. Next time we see Elen we'll tell him what we've found and he can check it out and tell mom and dad."

16

A Bungled Lynching

Jake has been furious for days because of Elen's refusal to move back in with him. He wants that reindeer and will go to any lengths to get him so he punched in Charlie's phone number.

"Hey, Charlie, I can't handle this frustration any longer. I have to get rid of that weasel, Elen, once and for all. I want that reindeer. Round up a dozen or so cowboys and bring an extra horse over for me. I'll need a couple of heavy duty ropes too."

"Sure, Jake, will do."

The next day as Elen was cooking he looked up to see Jake and a dozen cowboys.

"Awe jeez Jake, dog-gone-it, you're spoiling my dinner. I guess it wasn't clear that I didn't want to see you in the forest again and then you bring along a dozen other cowboys with you?"

"That ain't all that's gonna be spoiled. Boys' get him up on that horse, there's gonna be a hot time in the forest tonight," said Jake.

Ted lassoed Elen and several cowboys stepped up to put him on the horse but not before they tied a noose around his neck.

"Where do you want the hangin' done, boss?" asked Ted.

"Over yonder, under the large oak," said Jake as he pointed at the tree."

Ted led the horse to the oak. Wyatt climbed the tree and tied the rope around a large limb.

"Guess you boys didn't come over for a game of tiddly winks, huh?" asked Elen.

"Smart mouthed weasel. We're gonna be here to watch to make sure the job gets done this time."

"Hmmph, guess you'd call it show time, huh, Jake?"

"Yep, show time," said Jake. "Got any last words, weasel?"

"As a matter of fact, I do." Elen looked at Pere. "Pere, take those two over there in for a body wash." Elen nodded his head in the direction of two men. "It'll help lower my odds."

The two men looked at Elen like he was talking crazy and watched Pere fly into the air but they didn't expect to be picked up from the rear and carried off screaming. Pere flew them to the pond and dropped them in then returned to Elen.

As soon as Pere flew back, Jake hollered. "You boys corral that reindeer!"

The men went after Pere and he took to the sky. Coming in behind them, he picked up two more and hung them on a branch in the tree by their belt and returned for the others.

Jake watched dumbfounded as Pere delivered others to the top of the tree.

"So much for the cowboys huh, Jake?" asked Elen. "How much did you pay them?"

Jake got red in the face with anger. "Slap that rump," he hollered. The cowboy slapped the rump, Elen zapped the rope and the rope broke. Pere snickered.

"Oops, a rotten rope?" said Elen as he shrugged his shoulders.

"What the devil?" screamed Jake. "Get rid of that rope and get another around his neck, boys, and hurry it up," yelled Jake.

"Getting impatient, Jake?" asked Elen.

Damon tied another noose around Elen's neck and threw the end up to Ted. He tied it around the limb securely then climbed down.

"Don't know whether to wish you boys good luck or not," said Elen.

"Hit that rump," yelled Jake.

Ted slapped the horse's rump, Elen zapped the rope, the rope broke and Pere snickered louder.

"Ding dangit, Jake, you can't do anything right. I'm tired of playing cat and mouse your way. We're gonna play it my way this time. Pere, come hold this character for me." Elen jumped off the horse and grabbed Jake.

Pere held Jake by the belt with his antlers while Elen tied a noose around his neck and climbed the tree to tie it around the same limb. Elen pulled Jake's arms behind him and tied them. "Put him on the horse Pere; let's see how he likes it."

The cowboys' watch with bugged-out eyes and frozen in fear not knowing what their fate is going to be.

"What are you doing you idiot fool?" asked Jake. He looked up at the men in the tree. "You boys stop hangin' out up there. Get your rumps down here to help me out before this fool hangs me," yelled Jake.

Pere looked up at the men in the tree. They shrugged their shoulders as if to say *what do you expect us to do, Jake, fly?*

Elen walked over to Jake, "You got any last words, pardner?" asked Elen.

"Get me down from here you weasel. I'll have your head."

"Hmmph. That's all you have to say?" asked Elen. "Was that a threat or a promise?"

Sweat is rolling down Jake's face. His face is red and he's breathing hard, and is shaking like a leaf.

Jake looked up at the men in the tree. "Are you jackwagons' gonna let him do this and just watch while this weasel hangs me?"

"Some loyalty, Jake, I don't see any of them making an effort. Hope you didn't pay them too much. Looks like you're the one holding the bag," said Elen.

"Pere, let's head over to the pond to see if those boys are squeaky clean yet," said Elen.

"Wh-what? You gonna just leave me here like this? Wh-what if...." screamed Jake.

"Are you asking what if the horse bolts, or if a bee stings him on the rump, or if a cowboy falls out of the tree and spooks the horse? I don't know, Jake, you'll just have to take a chance. We'll be back, see ya soon....I think," said Elen.

Elen looked up at the men and watched them grab another limb to keep from falling. He smirked, shook his head, shrugged his shoulders and jumped on Pere and looked back at Jake.

"Sorry, Jake, old fella, that's the chance you have to take; the same chance you gave me."

"Come back here you low-life scoundrel. Don't leave me like this."

Pere flew off toward the pond. Elen could hear Jake's screams all the way to the pond.

When Elen and Pere arrived at the pond, the two men were struggling to get out.

"Oh, geez, you guys messed around and got stuck in the quicksand?" asked Elen. "Tsk, tsk, tsk, don't fight it, you'll sink deeper."

The men look up at Elen with a terrified look. "Th-This is quicksand?" asked one.

Elen nodded his head. "Yep, afraid so, it's slow, but deadly."

"Get us outta here," the other man screamed desperately. "Are you gonna sit there and watch us die, you fool?"

Elen laughed uproariously. "Who's the fool? The ones in the pond, or the one on the reindeer?"

"Okay, okay, we're the fools," screamed one of the cowboys. "Now, will you get us out of here?"

Elen slid off the Pere and crouched at the edge of the pond. "Now, if'n I do that, you just might come back and try to kill me again, so why should I worry?"

"No, no, we won't. That's a promise. We don't want anything to do with that snake, Jake, again."

"Did you hang Jake?" asked one of the cowboys?

"Well, let's just say he's hangin' in there …depends on if the horse decides to leave."

"Come on man, get us outta here."

"Well, I guess, I'll have to take your words for it. Pere, go over to see if you can lift them out. Who wants to go first?"

The men look at each other. "I-I… … …."

"Never mind, that's a tough decision. Pere, you decide." Pere flew to the one in black, lifted him with his antlers and took him to the edge of the pond then went after the other. Once they were out, they took off like a shot. Elen and Pere roared with laughter.

"Wanna go back to check on the others?" asked Pere.

"If you insist," said Elen.

When they arrived at the oak, Jake was still on the horse pouring with sweat, and shaking so hard he was having a hard time staying upright.

Pere looked at Elen. "Guess he didn't find a way out."

"Nope, I see you and the boys are still hanging in there, Jake. I figured you'd find a way to slip out of that rig," said Elen.

"You're going to be hanging from the other end of this rope if I ever get hold of you," threatened Jake.

"Now, Jake, don't talk like that. Didn't work both times you tried. You think the third time will be a charm?" asked Elen.

"I hope your soul rots," said Jake.

"Ohhh my, that's a dreadful thing to say. Problem is, if I have a soul, it has an everlasting life so I don't think it will be rotting. Well, Pere, we may as well get this over with."

"No, no, I don't wanna die," yelled Jake.

"You should have thought about that earlier."

Elen walked behind the horse, slapped him on the butt, zaps the rope, the rope breaks and the horse bolted. Jake was struggling to stay on. Elen and Pere laughed hysterically.

"I guess we should release the others, too, Pere," said Elen.

"Yeah, we'd better do it before they sprout wings."

Pere flew up to the tree and released the others one by one and they streaked out of the forest never to be seen again.

Jake slid off the horse when he reached his shack and tried to open the door with his hands tied behind his back; it was difficult. He kept trying until he finally got it open. He went to the kitchen for a knife and an hour later he was freed. He punched in Charlie's number.

"Where in the world did you find those worthless cowboys? I want that weasel gone and I don't care how we go about it. He has made a fool of me for the last time," screamed Jake.

"Calm down, Jake. They didn't expect the tables to be turned. You can't blame them. You didn't expect it either. We'll work on it until we get him," said Charlie.

"You're right; we'll get him and the reindeer. Get the word out I'm offering a ten thousand dollar reward for his capture," said Jake.

"Whoa, you'd go that far?"

"You bet I would."

"Okay, I'll spread the word," said Charlie.

As Elen lie down that night, he thought about the happening that day. He expected it to occur again and again. He knew now what Jake's intention was and that was to claim Pere as his own. How was he going to stop it? How was he going to protect Pere? He tossed and tumbled until early dawn before sleep overcame him.

Printed in the United States
by Baker & Taylor Publisher Services